SOPHIE PEMBROKE

I've been dreaming, reading and writing romance for years, ever since I stayed up all night devouring Harlequin Mills and Boon novels as part of my English degree, and promptly gave up any pretext of enjoying tragic stories. After all, what's the point of a book without a happy ending?

Born overseas, I grew up in Wales and now make my home in Hertfordshire with my scientist husband and our four year old, Alice in Wonderland obsessed, daughter. I keep a blog on my website, which should be about romance and writing, but is usually about cake and castles instead.

The Kiss Before Christmas

SOPHIE PEMBROKE

Harper*Impulse* an imprint of
HarperCollins*Publishers* Ltd
77–85 Fulham Palace Road
Hammersmith, London W6 8JB

www.harpercollins.co.uk

A Paperback Original 2014

First published in Great Britain in ebook format by Harper*Impulse* 2013

A catalogue record for this book
is available from the British Library

ISBN: 978-0-00-759177-0

Automatically produced by Atomik ePublisher from Easypress

For Charlotte.

I wouldn't be here without you.

Chapter 1

Dorothea Mackenzie stared at the screen, willing the words to change. They didn't. She tried blinking. Nope, still there, in all their guilt-trip-inducing glory.

> *My dearest Dory,*
> *We went to choose the Christmas tree yesterday, sweetheart,*
> *but it wasn't the same without you. I think Mum was a bit*
> *sad decorating it without any of you kids around, but Molly*
> *and Tim don't get in until the 24th, and she didn't want to*
> *leave it that late. She had 'Lonely This Christmas' playing*
> *on a loop. A call from you would definitely cheer her up –*
> *especially if you happened to mention your flight times (hint*
> *hint!). I can come and collect you from the airport any time*
> *on Christmas Eve, just let me know. I've not taken any taxi*
> *bookings the whole day, just in case.*
> *Love and mulled wine*
> *Dad x*

A definite two-pronged attack. Clever. First mentioning Mum being sad, which they all knew meant big eyes and deep sighs and very brave smiles, and which he knew Dory couldn't stand. And then not taking any bookings on Christmas Eve, a night that promised time-and-a-half for a Liverpool cabbie, and usually some pretty good festive tips, too.

All this despite the fact she'd told him a month and a half ago she wouldn't be home for Christmas. Hell, she'd already posted all their presents.

'They're bringing out the big guns now, then?' Tyler said, reading over her shoulder in that way he knew she hated. 'How are you going to get out of that one?'

Dory shifted her computer screen so he couldn't see. There wasn't a lot of point; she was pretty sure IT would send him up every email she'd ever received or sent if he asked. But it was the principle of the thing. 'Aren't bosses supposed to be less…' She trailed off still in search of the right word to describe Tyler.

'Charming? Handsome? Awesome?' he guessed.

'Intrusive.'

'Hmm. And I thought assistants were supposed to be more fawning, generally.' He wagged a finger at her, mock sternly. 'Don't think you can get away with anything, just because you've got that cute British accent thing going.'

Dory was starting to suspect that her accent was the only reason he'd hired her. It certainly wasn't to fawn over him, since she'd made it painfully clear at the job interview that that wasn't going to happen. In fact, the exact phrase she'd used was 'I'm not the kind of assistant who fetches your dry-cleaning and straightens your tie. I'm the kind of assistant who makes your workload lighter.'

Dad always said she wasn't great with subtle.

Of course, for the brief three-month period when she'd had an assistant of her own, back at her last job – her Dream Job – she hadn't exactly been fawned over either. More insulted, actually.

Maybe her assistant hadn't liked the accent. Liverpudlian was an acquired taste, Dory supposed.

'Was there something you actually wanted?' Dory asked. 'A report that needs writing, or a meeting to set up?'

'Yeah, I need you to pull up the publicity shots from that charity event in Washington D.C. last week. See what people are saying about the cause, the people involved, that sort of thing.'

'You mean you want me to check that they caught your best side in the photos.' She'd been Tyler's assistant for six months now. She knew what *really* mattered to him, and it often had little to do with the multi-million-dollar restaurant chain he stood to inherit, or its subsidiaries – even if he was the CEO.

'That too,' he admitted with a grin. 'Send them through when you've got them.'

He swept off back into his office and Dory turned to more important matters than whether or not Tyler's eyes looked red in some photos surely no one really cared about. Like how to break it to Dad that she really, really wasn't coming home for Christmas.

It wasn't that she didn't *want* to go back to good old Blighty. Her stomach rumbled at the very thought of Dad's Christmas dinner and Mum's mince pies. She was nostalgic about beating her siblings at Monopoly while they drank their way through a bucket of mulled wine until they all ended up writing each other IOUs for ridiculous sums of rent. She wanted a soggy Christmas-Day walk after the Queen's speech and turkey sandwiches while watching the Doctor Who Christmas Special.

But she couldn't.

Working for Tyler Alexander had a lot of perks, but unfortunately the pay wasn't one of them. It paid the rent, got her invited to some pretty cool parties, and provided the entertainment of working with Tyler, scion of the Alexander family and generally fun guy to be around. But it didn't stretch to holiday-period flights to the British Isles.

Of course, she couldn't tell Dad that. Especially since her parents still believed she was working at the aforementioned Dream Job.

She should have told them by now. It wasn't going to get any easier, after all. But she just hadn't found quite the right way to break it to them yet. And yeah, okay, maybe a part of her was still hoping she'd get back the life she moved to the States for, before anybody back home noticed that she'd let it slip through her fingers. Dream job, devoted, successful and *rich* fiancé, Manhattan penthouse apartment… Now she shared a shoebox of a flat an hour's commute away, put up with Tyler's daily demands (while still refusing to deal with his wardrobe in any way) and didn't even want to think about dating. And, as if that weren't enough to make her miserable, she couldn't go home for Christmas.

With a sigh, Dory pushed her chair up to the desk again and rested her hands on the keyboard. How was she going to do this?

She glanced at the office door. When in doubt, blame Tyler.

Dear Dad

I wish I was there to see the tree – send photos? And you know 'Lonely this Christmas' is Mum's favourite. She'd be listening to it even if I was there. Which, unfortunately, I'm not going to be able to be. You know there's nowhere else in the world I want to be on Christmas Day, but I'm afraid work is crazy and I can't get the time off to even fly there and back and say hi at the airport! Maybe in the New Year…

She stopped. Things weren't going to be any better in January, and there was no point pretending that they would.

Deleting the words, she clicked on to the Internet browser and brought up the travel website she used whenever Tyler needed to jet off somewhere at short notice. Typing 'New York' and 'London' into the starting point and destination fields, she held her breath while it did its magic.

When the price range appeared on the screen, she winced and closed the tab. No way. Even if she was willing to give up food and shelter for the foreseeable future, there wasn't enough money in her bank account to get her halfway across the ocean.

Her hand drifted to the locked top drawer of her desk entirely of its own accord. It knew what she kept there, hoping that the lock and key would protect her from temptation. She kept it at work so she didn't have it on hand in her weakest moments. Like late at night, watching QI repeats on her laptop with a large glass of wine, and feeling homesick.

In that drawer, tucked away behind her stationery supplies, was the emergency credit card her father had insisted she get before she'd left for New York with Ewen.

She'd never used it, but she knew the credit limit was high enough to get her a ticket home. She could use it, have a few days with friends and family, then return to New York with nobody any the wiser as to her current fall from perfection. It was an ideal solution – she'd keep up appearances and get to go home for Christmas.

Except she'd be paying off the trip for the rest of her life. And what would she do if there really was an emergency and she couldn't pull out the magic credit card to get her home?

Sighing, Dory pulled her hand away from the drawer. Dad had a rule about credit cards, one he'd drummed into her repeatedly before she left for university, and on every visit thereafter.

It's not an emergency unless someone is bleeding, or there's a real chance of decapitation.

She could probably get away with a more general risk of death than decapitation but still, neither applied in this case. The only thing at risk was her pride. And perhaps her relationship with her parents.

If she asked, if she confessed all, she knew Mum and Dad would try and find a way to pay for her to go home, but they didn't have the money any more than she did. And it would be a one-way trip. If she left New York, broke and desperate, she wouldn't be coming back. And she wasn't ready to give up just yet.

The phone rang in Tyler's office – never a good sign. The only person who had Tyler's direct line, and so didn't have to come through Dory, was his mother. She'd tricked it out of his previous assistant, which might have been why the job suddenly became available. And now Tyler couldn't change the number or his mother would know he was avoiding her.

Personally, Dory was just glad she didn't have to take the calls.

Within moments, a message from Tyler flashed up on her screen. *Get photos. Now!*

Dory rolled her eyes. Classic avoidance tactic. She would go in there, needing to urgently speak to him about photos, of all things, and he could legitimately tell his mother he had to go because something had come up.

Pulling up the search engine, she typed Tyler's name into the search box. Usually that was all it took to get the most recent articles and photos up. She'd narrow it down by venue and event if there were too many. But before she could click search, the phone rang.

'Tyler Alexander's office,' Dory said. 'How can I help you?'

'Is my brother there?' The voice was unfamiliar, even after six months of working for Tyler, but she could make an easy educated guess at its owner. Lucas Alexander. The black sheep.

'I'm sorry Mr Alexander, Tyler is on the phone right now.' What did he want? She supposed this was the time of year when estranged brothers might suddenly get in touch, if only to discuss what on earth to buy their mother – the original woman-who-has-everything – for Christmas.

'Let me guess – our mother.' He sounded almost amused. His voice was deeper than Tyler's, richer somehow.

'I believe it might be.' Dory clicked search then, while it was working, opened a new tab and typed the name 'Lucas Alexander' into the search bar. *Let's see exactly who I'm talking to.* 'Do you want me to ask Tyler to patch you in on a conference call with them?'

'God, no!' As Lucas spoke, a series of images began to load on Dory's screen, all several years old, and all gorgeous. Lucas Alexander in a suit, on his wedding day, in shorts and a t-shirt on some beach somewhere… and one, the most recent shot of him, two years ago, in a dark coat and sunglasses. She clicked on that one.

'In that case, can I take a message?' she asked. The new page loaded with the headline 'Alexander Drop Out?' Dory scrolled down. *CEO of the Alexander Corporation and heir to the family fortune, Lucas Alexander last night sensationally stepped down from the company, amid rumours of his divorce from socialite Cheryl Franklin.*

'If she's on the phone, then she's already seen the photos. I take it Tyler hasn't yet?' Lucas said.

'Photos?' Dory guiltily clicked back to the tab with the photos she was *supposed* to be looking for. 'Oh my.'

'Yeah. Not exactly the public image my dad usually likes us to promote for the Corporation.' Lucas sighed. 'It's going to be a long Christmas break. Look, tell him I tried to warn him, yeah?'

'I will,' Dory promised, eyes still glued to the screen and the phone still in her hand long after Lucas had hung up.

As the dial tone buzzed, she finally put it down. *Get it together, Dory.* She needed to figure out exactly what was going on here.

Okay, so to start with, those weren't photos from the latest charity gala. Dory was pretty sure he'd never have his hand that far up a woman's dress in front of the country's foremost do-gooders. She squinted at the picture on the screen. Who was she? No one Dory recognised, although the lighting and the woman's position made it hard to pick out much beyond dark hair and long legs. Which didn't narrow it down much. Tyler had what you might call A Type. Every woman she'd ever seen him out with had dark hair and long legs.

Hell, *she* had dark hair and reasonably lengthy legs. It could be her, except she'd never get that up-close-and-personal with her boss. She liked a guy with a little more depth, thanks.

A guy unlike her ex, as it turned out.

Although, now she thought about it, while she'd seen Tyler with a variety of women on his arms over the last six months, she'd never seen him with the same one twice. And she'd never seen him look at one like he could barely stop himself touching her, cameras be damned.

Whoever the woman in these photos was, she mattered to him. And he really wasn't going to like the world seeing that. Let alone his mother…

Dory clicked on the article that went with the photos, checking the date stamp and scanning the text. The usual words popped out – *Alexander family scion, billionaire, most eligible* – but this time her eye stopped and paid attention to the second paragraph.

Usually seen in public with exactly the right woman for the occasion, accessorising his charity galas, publicity events and even dinner invitations like he'd match his tie to his suit, Tyler Alexander has never been afraid to show off his companions. Which makes us wonder about this one! Who is she? Where did they meet? Why is he keeping her a secret? And – could it be because, at last, Tyler has found The One?

Oh dear. Oh dear, oh dear, oh dear. He really wasn't going to like this. Apart from anything else, it might give the girl expectations – something Tyler studiously tried to avoid.

She looked at the picture again. Maybe this one really was different, though. In which case he'd probably be up in arms about invasion of privacy. Some days, you really couldn't win with Tyler.

Reluctantly, she emailed him the link, then waited. Not for very long, mind. Within a minute, there was a reply.

GET IN HERE NOW!

He was still on the phone to his mother, so Dory slipped through the door and sat very, very quietly in the visitor's chair on the other side of his desk. The chances of him not noticing she was there were slim, especially since he'd ordered her in, but she figured it was worth a try. She took a moment to remind herself that this *was not* her fault. She hadn't been on a date with a strange woman, or got caught. She hadn't even been responsible for making the dinner reservation, since she hadn't even known he'd gone. She was in no way responsible for this. It was important to remember this – these things had a tendency to become completely irrelevant when Tyler was in a snit and looking for someone to blame.

'I can't just… she might have plans, Mother.' Tyler slumped back in his chair, his eyes closed. 'Yes, we've talked about… I'm sure she'd…' He sighed. Dory sympathised; getting a word in edgeways when talking to Felicia Alexander was clearly not easy. 'Mother. I'll ask her, okay? I don't know what else you want me to do.' Stupid question. Tyler went silent again as his mother presumably gave him a list. 'Fine. I'll ask. Goodbye, Mother.'

Throwing the phone at the desk, he reached up to rub his temples. Dory, more concerned about his mother eavesdropping on whatever conversation followed, picked up the receiver and put it back on the hook. Then she sat back and waited for the blame to fall.

'How could you let them post that picture?' Tyler pointed at her, eyes open and accusing now.

'How could you let them take it?' she countered. 'And it's a bit hard to pull photos of you I don't even know exist, out with a woman I didn't know you were dating, on an evening I didn't even know you were out.'

After six months, he followed that ramble of thought without too much trouble. One of the reasons she liked working for him.

Tyler sighed. 'Yeah, okay. I screwed up. It's just…'

'She matters to you?' Dory guessed, when he paused.

A sharp, short nod was the only acknowledgement she got. 'But she is *not* a woman I can take home to meet the family over the holidays.'

Why not? Dory didn't ask, because making Tyler madder didn't seem like a good to-do list item for the day, but she couldn't help but come up with some answers on her own. Was she a prostitute? The daughter of a business rival? His ex? Or just someone who'd be deemed unsuitable by the Alexander family at large? That probably took up most of the population.

'Your mother wants you to take her home to Midfield House for Christmas?'

Tyler groaned and nodded. 'Apparently it's the only socially acceptable thing to do after you appear in a compromising photo with a woman, and it's plastered all over the Internet.'

'Of course.' Only Felicia Alexander would have a book of etiquette for this situation. Tyler always said that because the Alexanders were only old-ish money, with their first restaurant opened in the early twentieth century, rather than old nineteenth-century industrialist money, his mother always felt she had to be even more proper than proper. 'So what're you going to do?'

Dory leant forward, resting her elbows on his desk, and stared across at him. Tyler Alexander under pressure; often when he did his best work, she'd found.

But apparently not today. He sighed and rubbed a hand across his forehead. 'Call my lawyer, I suppose. See if we can cut some sort of deal with the magazine in question before the pictures make it from online to print. Get them to take them down, maybe. Break a leg so I don't have to go home for Christmas.'

He was joking, of course. Even if he didn't look like it. But just in case... 'Don't say that. It'll be your own fault if you slip on the pavement on the way to catch a cab to the train station.'

'Sidewalk,' Tyler corrected her. Dory sighed. He was determined to make her a real American, one colloquialism at a time.

'Besides, home is where you're supposed to be for the holidays. Holidays are for family.'

Tyler's gaze jerked up to meet hers. 'You're not going home,' he pointed out.

Dory sank backwards with a sigh, thinking of the email she still had to send to Dad. 'I would if I could. It's just... not possible.'

'Because...?'

'Because you don't pay me enough,' she said, smirking at him. It was a familiar argument. Of course, the truth was, even a hefty pay rise would be swallowed up by frivolous expenses like food and heating. Basic living expenses were extreme in New York. She'd thought, coming from London, she'd be used to it. But in London she'd had the ex to share the bills with. Of course, she'd thought she'd be sharing with him in New York, too…

'What if I could arrange for you to go home for New Year?' Tyler asked. The gleam in his eye told her there'd be a catch, but the surge of excitement that coursed through her overwhelmed any caution.

'Really? That would be… God, that would be fantastic.' It wasn't Christmas, of course, but it was a damn sight better than nothing. Her parents might even still be speaking to her by the time she got there if she could mollify them with a trip home at the end of the month.

'I'll book you a ticket,' Tyler promised, smiling beatifically. 'If you spend Christmas with my family.'

Chapter 2

Dory froze. 'Wait. What?'

'Spend Christmas up at the family estate with me, and I'll arrange for you to go home for New Year,' Tyler said. 'It's pretty straightforward, Dory.'

No it wasn't. Because she'd spotted the catch. 'Spend Christmas with you in what capacity, exactly?'

He must have heard the suspicion in her voice, because he winced. 'As my fake girlfriend.'

Not just a catch. A ginormous, all-encompassing Catch with a capital C. 'Not a chance.'

'You haven't heard the whole plan. At least hear me out,' Tyler said, holding up his hands. 'Besides, weren't you the one who said that holidays are for family?'

'I didn't mean yours!'

'Better than being stuck here in a strange city, all alone...'

'I'm not completely sure of that.' Spending Christmas with the Alexander family seemed infinitely more intimidating. They probably wore tuxes for dinner every single night. Dory had mastered the whole which-cutlery-to-use-first thing when she dated the son of an MP at university, but beyond that? She'd be lost. And they probably wouldn't let her illegally stream Doctor Who on Christmas Day, either.

'Come on, Dory.' He was using his persuasive voice now. Never a good sign. 'Think about it. You get a luxury, catered Christmas break, followed by an all-expenses-paid trip back home for New Year. And all you have to do is look adoringly at me for a few days.'

'They'll never buy it,' she said. 'Your mother has spoken to me on the phone. She'll recognise my voice.' Not to mention Lucas. She knew she'd recognise his voice again anywhere. She'd be kind of disappointed if he didn't recognise hers.

'She's spoken to you precisely twice,' Tyler said. 'I don't think she pays that much attention to my assistants.'

'Still. Do you really think they'll believe that you're dating…' She paused. Why wouldn't they? She was young, attractive, exactly his type and, most importantly, awesome. 'Do you really think they'll believe I'd date you?'

Tyler laughed, a deep, belly laugh. At least she'd managed to cheer him up. 'Bear in mind, they think I'm hiding my girlfriend from them.'

'Which you are.'

'So they have to imagine there'd be a reason.'

'Like… me being British?' If he seriously wanted her to consider this proposition, he had to admit all the reasons it probably wouldn't work. Of which, her nationality was the least important. She wasn't part of his society, part of his world. That was the part no one was going to believe.

'Like you being my assistant.'

Ah, yes. That. Dory winced. 'So, we're going to tell them that?'

Tyler's gaze slid away from hers. 'Maybe, maybe not. But if they figure it out… it's plausible as a story, anyway.'

'Wouldn't it be easier just to take your actual girlfriend?'

'Believe it or not, no.' Tyler looked suddenly tired. 'Look, I know it's probably a disaster waiting to happen. But it's the best idea I've got. Otherwise I'm going to be spending the entire Christmas break with my extended family asking constant questions about my personal life, questions that I really cannot answer, and I'm right back to the "breaking a leg plan" just to get away from them.'

Dory tipped her head back and considered the ceiling for a while. On the one hand, this was clearly a very stupid idea. She'd watched the rom-coms. She knew how this ended – with everyone finding out about the deception in the most humiliating and public way possible, and hating her forever. But then, she had a few advantages over all those movie heroines.

1) She wasn't in love with her boss, and there was absolutely no chance of her falling in love with her boss. She knew him too well.

2) Her boss wasn't secretly in love with her, thank God. In fact, he seemed pretty taken with someone else.

3) She didn't actually care if the Alexander family hated her. Hell, Felicia probably already did, despite only talking to her twice. Once again, probably the accent.

So, given those facts, what was she risking, really? And was spending New Year with her family – and keeping up the illusion of her perfect life in front of her nearest and dearest – worth the risk?

'Do you promise that whatever happens I won't lose my job?' Dory asked.

'Absolutely. You're unexpectedly and inexplicably the best assistant I've ever had.' Tyler looked too confused by the fact for her to take this as an actual compliment. 'After the holidays, we'll just decide that we're better as friends, or we need to keep things professional, or something.'

Yeah, that sounded well thought out. But since the break-up would be his problem, as long as she still had her job at the end of it, Dory wasn't too worried.

'And you'll fly me business class back home in time for New Year? And give me two weeks' holiday there?' May as well push the boat out, she figured.

Tyler raised an eyebrow. 'If that's what you want. Personally, two weeks seems far too long to spend with family, but who am I to question the English way? So you'll do it? Spend three days with my family and faithfully swear to be the woman in the photos?

And – this is important – not ask questions?'

Dory bit her lip. No questions? She didn't like the sound of that. 'No questions at all?'

'Not if you want the trip.'

She should demand to know who the other woman was, why he couldn't take her. But she really wanted to go home for New Year…

'Do you snore?'

'I said no questions.'

Dory sighed. 'I'm in.'

***

Two days later, late afternoon on December 23rd, Dory rolled her suitcase out of the lift – no, sorry Tyler, *elevator* – straight past her desk and into Tyler's office. She'd negotiated the day off to prepare for the horrors ahead. But now it was nearly time to go and Tyler was still working.

He glanced up as she entered, but his attention went right back to his paperwork the moment he realised it was only her. That kind of attitude wasn't going to convince anyone that he was madly in love with her. The man in that photo had looked considerably more besotted.

'I'm guessing the perfect boyfriend act doesn't start until we actually get there, then?' she said, dropping into the chair opposite his desk. His suitcase was propped up against the wall in the corner of the office, which was something.

'Mmmhmm.' He didn't even look up that time. How had the idiot ever got so many women to fall for him in the first place?

'I've got the train times here,' she told him. He worked on, oblivious. 'Want me to try and reserve seats? Or just get tickets at the station?'

No response.

'I'll call a cab to Grand Central, shall I?'

Nothing. This did not bode well for the journey north.

She sighed. 'So the chances of getting you to carry my suitcase out to the cab are—'

'Slim.' That wasn't Tyler. The word came from the doorway, in a deeper, warmer, far more amused voice. A voice she recognised. Dory wondered how much Lucas had heard. Hopefully not the perfect boyfriend crack. She winced. She really was going to have to be more careful.

Tyler had jerked to attention the moment his brother spoke. Dory rolled her eyes. Of course he looked up *now*. 'Lucas.'

Something about the way he said the name sounded off. But Dory didn't dwell on it too long. Not when Lucas Alexander, the black sheep himself, was standing right behind her. Her curiosity had much better things to do than ponder about Tyler's big brother issues.

Instead, she swivelled the chair around, plastered on her best 'meet the family' smile, and got gracefully to her feet. Well, mostly gracefully. She only had to grab the arm of the chair a little bit, and she didn't think that Lucas noticed. Much.

'Hi! I'm Dory,' she said, letting go of the chair and wobbling forward. Probably the fault of the heels on her new knee-high boots. Because Lucas, though tall, broad, and smiling that same Alexander smile that had been plastered all over the Internet that week, wasn't nearly as classically handsome as his brother, and she worked with Tyler five days a week without swooning even a little bit. Which wasn't to say that Lucas wasn't attractive, of course. Better looking than his photos, even. Just… with rougher edges than his younger brother.

Maybe it was the stubble.

'So you're who he's bringing home to meet Mother.' Lucas ran his eyes from her perfectly straightened and shiny hair, past her respectable yet stylish, seasonally green dress, to the aforementioned polished boots. Dory waited him out. She knew how to dress for a part. In the end, his gaze flicked over to Tyler instead, and she chalked a mental point up to her side. She wasn't entirely sure what the competition was, yet, but there was no mistaking the challenge in Lucas's gaze. What was it? she wondered. Checking to see if she was good enough for his brother? Or did he have his own suspicions about who Tyler was with the other night? Why else had he suddenly shown up here, when as far as she was aware, he was supposed to already be up at the family estate, dancing attendance on Felicia?

Tyler darted out from behind his desk at last, standing midway between her and Lucas, glancing between them, obviously caught off-guard by his brother's arrival.

'Lucas, this is Dorothea. My girlfriend.' He didn't even choke on the last couple of words. She was almost proud.

'Dory,' she corrected him.

The smile Tyler gave her was far more charming, more affectionate than she'd ever seen from him before. Apparently the perfect boyfriend act was on, at last.

'Darling, you know I prefer your full name. Far more beautiful. Just like you.'

Yeah, they were screwed. Nobody was going to fall for this. Ever.

But in the doorway, Lucas merely rolled his eyes. 'Well, if you two lovebirds are ready, we may as well get this show on the road.'

'Show?' Dory asked. 'I was just about to call for a cab to the station…'

Lucas shook his head. 'Not anymore. Mother decided there were far too many ways a train journey could get delayed, or even cancelled. So I'm driving us all up there. Together.'

***

Lucas didn't wait to see the annoyance on his brother's face. Bad enough he was being sent to play fetch because Mother's insecurities, paranoia and control issues had reached a new height. He wasn't pandering to his brother's fragile ego too. He didn't care who Tyler was dating, besides a fleeting thought that Mother would hate the heels on those boots. Lucas quite liked that thought and the way the boots clung to Dory's calves, but beyond that he didn't really care if she came for Christmas or not. Personally, Lucas wasn't all that bothered about being there for Christmas himself. In and out, that was his plan. Stay just long enough to mollify Mother for another few months, then get the hell out of town, back to his real life. The one that didn't involve the Alexander legacy anymore.

Except… the thing with the photos. Something about it felt off. Like Tyler was hiding something. And if there was a problem, Lucas really needed to get it fixed before their parents figured out what it was and used it as another excuse to try and drag Lucas back into the family business. He'd only got out in the first place because Tyler was there, ready and eager to step into the CEO role – and had already proved himself capable while Lucas was in the hospital. But Patrick Alexander believed in the proper way of doing things, and Lucas knew that not having his eldest son in charge of the company still rankled. Mostly because he kept telling him so. And if he got it into his head that Tyler was a liability to the family reputation…

Lucas shook the thought away. Tyler was fine. He had Dory to present to his parents and a few unfortunate photos would soon be forgotten. It would all be okay.

He just had to get through a two-hour drive north from New York on the busiest Friday of the year, with his brother and his latest flame in the car with him, then survive three days with his family.

Easy.

'You guys ready to go?' Lucas jangled the keys in his hand in the hope they'd get the hint. Getting out of Manhattan on the Friday before Christmas would be a nightmare as it was. If they waited much longer they were bound to catch the worst of the traffic.

'Yeah. Yeah, sure,' Tyler said, but he slid back behind his desk as he spoke. 'I just need to…' he trailed off as his gaze caught on the paperwork again.

Lucas gave Dory a meaningful glance. Surely this was girlfriend territory if ever he'd seen it.

She looked confused for a moment, but then she sighed. Stepping towards the desk on those ridiculous heels, she leant over, giving Lucas a stunning view of her ass. Blinding her boyfriend with cleavage to get her way, he supposed. He sighed. *Aren't you bored of that kind of girl yet, Tyler?*

But then Dory grabbed the file in front of Tyler and, straightening up, flicked through it, then closed it. 'This can wait until we get back. Mr Jenkins is away until the New Year now, anyway.' She grabbed the next file in the stack. 'This became irrelevant after yesterday's late meeting, and this one I dealt with last week.' Picking up the last two files on the desk she gave them a cursory glance and said, 'If you're very good, I might let you take these two with you. But you're only allowed to work first thing in the morning, before any of your family gets up. Deal?'

Okay, maybe this was a different sort of girl.

'But Dory,' Tyler whined, but she cut him off.

'No arguing. That's the deal, okay? If I'm with your family, you're with your family.' She handed the permitted files across the desk to him. 'Now let's get going before we hit the traffic. Since we have such a considerate ride to your parents' house.'

She turned back and beamed at Lucas then, but he didn't smile back. He'd finally put his finger on what had been bothering him about Dory since he walked in. The accent. How had he not placed it before? After all, he'd heard it just a few days earlier.

'You're his assistant,' he said. And there it was. The scandal that Tyler was hiding from their family-first, believer-in-good-old-fashioned-morals father.

Dory's smile faltered, but only for a moment. Then she glared at Tyler. 'Told you someone would notice.'

'Lucas can keep a secret. Can't you, bro?' Tyler said.

Three days of keeping secrets from his parents. Just what he'd wanted from his brother for Christmas. 'That's why you were hiding her. Why the photos were such a big deal. Why you didn't want to…'

'Didn't want to bring me home to meet the family,' Dory finished for him when he trailed off awkwardly. 'It's okay. I know I'm not exactly the sort of girlfriend Tyler usually brings home. There's the accent, apart from anything else.'

'On the plus side, you seem much better at telling him what to do,' Lucas offered, making her grin. She had a nice smile, he realised. Wide and bright and friendly. Which wouldn't get her anywhere with Patrick and Felicia Alexander.

Then she scowled at Tyler. 'I am. So get in the car, Alexander!'

Grabbing her own case, Dory headed for the lift again, but Lucas stopped her. 'I'll take that for you.'

He held out a hand and, after a moment's pause, Dory let go of the handle and pushed the case towards him. 'Nice to know one of you Alexander boys is a gentleman,' she said, in a terrible impression of a Southern-belle drawl.

Tyler's laugh was louder than Lucas thought it really needed to be. 'Oh trust me,' he said, 'Lucas opted out of gentleman status two years ago. Besides, I've got my own case to carry.' He held it up, as if to prove the point.

But Dory wasn't looking at her boyfriend. She was looking at Lucas, and the curiosity on her face made him nervous.

'And why was that, exactly?' she asked. 'Tyler never really talks about his family. Well, not as people, anyway.'

'Hey! What's that supposed to mean?' Tyler asked, as Lucas headed for the lift, case in hand.

He knew what Dory meant, even if Tyler didn't. To Tyler, the family was the Alexander Family and all the restaurants, charity and money that went with it, not the individuals who were born into it. It was sort of inevitable, he supposed. The reputation of the family, their success, had always been the measuring stick of their parents' happiness and pride.

It had been Lucas's, too, until two weeks in a hospital one fall taught him different.

Dory didn't answer Tyler's question, which he figured gave him permission not to answer hers, either. But he had a feeling it was going to be a long car journey.

***

Dory stared at the mud-smeared wheels and side of the four-wheel drive, looking utterly out of place parked in front of the Alexander Building offices.

'I'm guessing you don't live in the city, then?' she said, as she followed Lucas and her suitcase around to the boot of the car. No, not boot. Trunk. One day, she'd get that right and someone would appear and announce her a true American, once and for all.

Tyler laughed. 'City life is one of the many things Lucas has scorned over the last couple of years.' Leaving his case by the back of the car, he went to climb into the passenger seat. Dory pulled a face. Great. Two hours in the back of the car would do nothing for the butterflies in her stomach. Chances were, she'd arrive at Midfield House and immediately vomit all over a poor, defenceless servant. Or worse, Felicia Alexander herself.

'Hey, Tyler? In the back.' Dory looked over at Lucas as he spoke, but he slammed the boot and climbed into the driver's seat. Weirdly, it seemed like her fake boyfriend's brother was on her side.

'I've got longer legs,' Tyler argued. 'I need the room.'

'I get car sick,' Dory told him, yanking open the passenger-side door. 'Trust me, we're all going to be happier with me in the front.'

'Fine.' Looking sulkier than a billionaire businessman and heir to one of the most profitable family businesses in the country had any right to, Tyler clambered back out of the front seat and into the back.

'Thank you, darling,' Dory said, as sweetly as she could. Lucas smirked as she clipped on her seatbelt, waiting until she was settled before he started the engine.

Music blared out of the stereo, but Lucas made no move to

21

turn down the volume. Dory ducked her head to hide her smile as Freddie Mercury belted out 'Good Old-Fashioned Lover Boy.'

But Lucas obviously saw it anyway. 'You're a Queen fan?'

'My father is. He sings this song to my mother when he's doing the ironing on a Sunday.'

'Your father irons?' Tyler asked, sticking his head between the front seats.

'Your parents are still in Britain?' Lucas asked at the same time.

Dory decided to answer the more sensible question. 'Liverpool, yeah. I'm going back to see them over New Year.' She couldn't help the small glance back at Tyler as she spoke. He'd promised her the ticket as a present on Christmas morning at Midfield House. Until she had it in her hand, it still seemed impossible.

'Liverpool,' Lucas repeated. 'The Beatles, yeah?'

'Amongst other things.'

'Like?'

Dory looked up at him. 'Sorry?'

'Like what other things?' Lucas's gaze flicked away from the road as he smiled at her, then back again as he pulled out into the busy traffic.

'Um, the docks. Liverpool FC. The Liver building.'

'The accent.' Tyler's inflection made it clear that wasn't a compliment.

Dory glared at him between the seats. 'You always said my accent was the first thing you fell for about me, *darling*.'

The pointed endearment obviously reminded him of their arrangement and he recovered quickly. 'Yours isn't true Liverpudlian anymore, honey. It's mellowed. And on you, any accent would be beautiful.'

'Hmm. Better.' Dory settled back into her seat.

The stereo switched to 'Crazy Little Thing Called Love' and Tyler groaned.

'Do we really have to listen to this?' he asked. Dory and Lucas ignored him.

'In about five miles he's going to ask if we're nearly there yet,' Lucas told her. 'And another five after that he'll probably need a bathroom break.'

'Trust me, I know,' Dory said. 'He's dreadful in airports, too. Every time they call our flight he's disappeared off to do something.' Business trips with Tyler were a nightmare.

'He's even worse in cars,' Lucas replied. 'No in-flight entertainment.'

'I'm sitting right here, you know,' Tyler put in from the backseat. 'Ears burning.'

'I can't imagine you taking a lot of family road trips as kids,' Dory admitted. 'I'd have imagined more private planes and first-class travel.'

'Mostly, yeah,' Lucas said. 'But when we went away to school or came home for the holidays, our parents would send a car to get us. Tyler was always bored within the first twenty minutes.'

'Not everyone can be entertained by staring out of a window at nothing,' Tyler said. 'And seriously. Can we put some talk radio on or something?'

'Oh!' Dory rummaged around in her handbag and pulled out her iPod. 'I brought music!'

Lucas nodded at the car stereo. 'Then put it on.'

Plugging the iPod into the adapter, Dory scrolled through to the right playlist then sat back and waited, trying not to smile too much. No point giving away the surprise too early.

As Cliff Richard sang about seasonal plants and alcohol, Tyler buried his face in his hands.

'What, exactly, did I do to deserve this?' he asked.

Lucas winced at the music. 'Tyler, this is all your fault. Every last bit of it.'

Dory grinned and snuggled into the comfy car seat to try and nap for a while, the music of her traditional family Christmas all around her.

Chapter 3

'She's asleep,' Tyler said, reaching through the seats to prod his girlfriend's arm. 'Trust me, once she's out like that she's dead to the world for the next hour. You can turn off the music from hell.'

'I like it,' Lucas lied. 'It's festive.' They'd had a tour of traditional British Christmas pop music over the last quarter of an hour, some Lucas recognised, some he didn't. He supposed maybe you needed to have grown up with the songs to appreciate them properly. He liked the one about being lonely this Christmas, though, even if it made him wish he would be. Just him and his farm and his dog. TV, whisky and something simple for dinner.

Okay, he'd probably miss the food at Midfield House, if he was honest. But great food he could get at his own restaurant, and the company he could definitely live without.

'You're punishing me for something,' Tyler said. 'What?'

Lucas frowned at the dark road through the windscreen. 'Why would I be punishing you?' They hadn't spoken in months. The closest they'd got was when he phoned to warn him about the photos and spoken to Dory. He glanced over at her, asleep beside him. She looked surprisingly peaceful and relaxed, given what was waiting for them at the end of their drive.

'For the photos, maybe?' Tyler said. He sounded guilty. 'Or dating my assistant?'

24

'Since when have I cared who you date, Tyler?' Even if Dory could be something of a scandal. The press loved a good seducing-the-help story when it came to their financial or moral leaders. And between the restaurant business and the charitable arm, the Alexander Corporation was both. But Lucas was less bothered about the family and company reputations than he was about spending the next three days listening to his father and Tyler trying to find a way to spin it, while his mother tried to convince him to come back and run the company again.

'Never.' Tyler flopped back against the seat. His relief made Lucas nervous. Was there more to this story? What wasn't Tyler telling him? 'That's true.'

'So why would I be punishing you? Mother, on the other hand...'

'God, don't.' Tyler groaned. 'This is going to be a disaster, isn't it?'

'Probably.' But then Lucas remembered Dory insisting that Tyler leave work behind to spend time with his family. 'Maybe not for you, though. She might actually be good for you, this one.'

'Mum's going to hate her.'

'Our mother would hate anyone you brought home,' Lucas pointed out. Tyler was the beloved angel son. No woman stood a chance.

'She liked Cheryl,' Tyler said, and Lucas winced involuntarily at the mention of his ex-wife. Tyler was right. Lucas secretly believed that, if she'd been given a choice, Felicia would have kept Cheryl over him in the divorce.

'Cheryl was different,' he said, even though the fact she'd been so exactly the same as the rest of his family was the reason he'd had to divorce her in the end. 'Mum practically hand-picked her. She's the daughter of her best friend. She was planning the wedding before our third date. Besides, she was marrying me, not you. That makes a difference.'

'So you think if I married Cheryl, Mum would suddenly hate her?' Tyler asked.

Lucas met his brother's eye in the rear-view mirror, until Tyler glanced away. 'Are you likely to?'

'God no!' Tyler laughed. 'I mean, I'm with Dory.'

'Then can we stop talking about my ex-wife?'

'Absolutely.'

In the silence that followed, Dory's playlist clicked on to Elvis singing about his Blue Christmas. Lucas was willing to place money that the collective Alexander Christmas would be worse. *Elvis should be grateful to be alone.*

***

Chris Rea was singing about driving home for Christmas. Hadn't they already had that one? Dory blinked the sleep out of her eyes and winced as she straightened up in her seat.

'Where are we?' she asked, clearing her throat when the words came out croaky.

'About five minutes from Midfield House,' Lucas replied. 'You have good timing. Unlike your boyfriend.'

Nearly there. Nearly time. Her heart kicked up to double speed. They were really going to do this.

Dory peeked between the seats. Tyler obviously wasn't too nervous about the whole affair. Slumped across the length of the back seat, he was fast asleep, one arm across his face. 'He's not wearing his seatbelt.'

'I'm not going to crash. I wouldn't worry.'

But she did. Even though she wasn't actually his girlfriend, only an employee, and even though he wasn't actually breaking any law in the state of New York... he should still be wearing his damn seatbelt. If they were in Britain, he would be.

Lucas was wearing his, though. At least one of them had a brain.

'Haven't we had this song already?' Dory reached for the iPod. It was set to repeat.

'We've had all of them already. Some of them twice. Interesting mix you have there.'

'It's what we'd be listening to if I was at home right now,' Dory said, homesickness pulling at her stomach again. 'You could have turned it off.'

Lucas shrugged, and Dory couldn't help but admire the way his shoulders moved under his sweater, and how he steered the car with the barest touch from the one hand holding it. 'I figured that with you asleep, your music was the closest I was going to get to finding out about you.'

'You wanted to find out about me?' Dory twisted in her seat to get a better look at him. 'Why?'

He gave her a look that suggested he was re-evaluating her intelligence. 'Because you're dating my brother.'

'And do you always show such interest in your brother's girl-friends? Because I would imagine that would involve actually calling or staying in touch, something that, as far as I'm aware, you haven't done much of over the last six months.' Ha. That showed him.

But Lucas didn't even have the good grace to look a little guilty at the accusation. 'He's not usually dating his assistant.'

Oh yeah. That. Not for the first time, Dory found herself wondering how truly inappropriate Tyler's new girlfriend had to be for 'I'm dating my assistant' to be a better line to potentially have to feed to the family. And, oh God, maybe even the press. How long was he expecting this to drag on for? Who were they going to have to tell?

She really must get better at asking more questions before agreeing to something. This was exactly how she ended up broke and alone in New York in the first place. Ewen said 'It'll be fun! An adventure. You've always wanted to be more adventurous,' and she'd moved her whole life, lock, stock and barrel, all the way across the ocean with barely a backwards glance. Sometimes, she wondered if she'd only done it to live up to his expectation of her. Because, really, she hadn't ever wanted to be more adventurous. She'd been exactly the right amount of adventurous already, thank you.

And now she was here. Pretending to be the girlfriend of one of America's most eligible bachelors.

Even Ewen would have to admit this was an adventure and a half.

'Are you…' She paused, then started again. 'Will it be a problem, do you think? The assistant thing? If… when people find out?'

'Depends.' Lucas, it seemed, was a man of few words. Another way he was utterly different to his brother.

'On what?' If she were going to be his pretend-sister-in-law-to-be for the next few days, he'd have to get used to answering questions.

But Lucas just shrugged again. 'Lots of things.'

Refusing to get distracted by what were, even in the dark of the car, really quite spectacular shoulders, Dory pressed on. 'Like?'

He sighed. 'You. Him. Our father. Mother. The press. Whether you get married.'

Dory coughed violently at the last suggestion, suddenly sorry she'd asked. But the noise woke up Tyler, who lurched upright as Lucas took a right turn.

'What?' he asked, obviously only half awake.

'Nothing,' Lucas said. 'Dory and I were just discussing your future wedding.'

Of course *now* he wanted to chat. Dory glanced across. Was he smirking? Damn him. Well, if he thought one embarrassing moment would stop her asking questions this week, he was sadly mistaken.

But Tyler wasn't really listening, it seemed. He peered out of the window. 'Are we there?'

'Just turned on to the drive,' Lucas confirmed.

'Drive?' Dory asked, confused. This was a drive? They'd already been on it for half a mile or more.

'Mum doesn't like to get too close to the ordinary people. And Dad likes to hunt in the woods around the house,' Tyler explained.

'Trust me, it's better that they're out here in the middle of nowhere,' Lucas added. He stared straight out of the windscreen, but Dory got the impression he could drive this route with his eyes closed.

They driveway grew smoother, and rustic iron street lamps appeared at regular intervals on either side of the road. In the flashes of light, Dory could see the tension in Lucas's jaw, the way his hands gripped the steering wheel too tight. *He really doesn't want to be here.*

Why? She didn't know much about Lucas beyond what she'd read in articles about the Alexander family after he called. She knew he'd run the company after his father retired until, two years ago, he handed over the reins to Tyler. Since then, no one really knew what he'd been doing, it seemed. Which was strange. Famous, rich, attractive and talented men usually found their way into the headlines one way or another.

The only thing that had been reported about him was his divorce. Was that why he'd left the company? Heartbreak? Dory's nose wrinkled. It didn't seem likely. Lucas didn't seem like the kind of guy to let anything affect his life that strongly unless he chose it himself.

It was strange, though. Most of the photos that had run with the story had been the usual staged wedding shots. Man in tux, beautiful brunette in designer dress, lots of smiles. But the man in those photos was barely recognisable as the Lucas who'd showed up at the office to drive them to Midfield House, yet Dory couldn't quite put her finger on just what was different.

The car started to slow, and Dory stopped wondering about Lucas Alexander and focused instead on wondering what the hell she'd been thinking of agreeing to this.

Pulling on the handbrake, Lucas jumped out to fetch the bags from the boot. Tyler, back in character as the perfect boyfriend, came round to open her door.

'You ready for this?' he asked.

'Not remotely.' Dory grabbed her iPod from the dock, then

swung her legs out of the car, knees together, the way you were supposed to but she never did.

Tyler gave her a quick grin then, unexpectedly, a brotherly kiss on the top of her head. 'You'll be awesome. That's why I hired you, remember?'

'I don't remember this being in the job description,' Dory grumbled.

But it was too late to argue, because just then the front door to Midfield House opened, splashing light out on to the drive and revealing Felicia and Patrick Alexander waiting for them on the steps.

Dory swallowed. Show time.

***

Lucas stared up at his childhood home and wondered, not for the first time, how he'd ever survived growing up there.

'You're here!' His mother came down the steps, arms open wide, welcoming and expectant as only the perfect hostess could be. Lucas hung back as she hugged Tyler, then turned to his new girlfriend. 'And you must be Dory! Tyler has told us next to nothing about you, naughty boy. We're looking forward to finding out *everything*. Now, come on inside before you catch a chill. Come on, Lucas!' she called back, almost as an afterthought.

'Son.' His father gave him a nod as he walked past and Lucas returned it.

'Dad.'

There. That was all the family tenderness taken care of for one weekend, anyway.

Patrick clapped Tyler on the back as they all lingered in the oversized hallway. Dropping the bags to the floor, Lucas had a sudden, irrational fear that all the holly and ivy decking the curving bannisters might start growing overnight, trapping them all inside this monstrosity of a house for a hundred years, like Sleeping

30

Beauty. He shook the thought away.

'So, where have you been hiding this beauty then, Tyler?' Patrick asked. Lucas was pretty sure his dad was going for friendly and welcoming with his smile, but Dory looked uncomfortable under it. Lucas could sympathise. Studied attention from his father had never ended well for him, either.

'He wasn't hiding me, exactly. Just… we didn't… well…' Dory tripped over her words, obviously trying to soften her accent, and Lucas winced. She was nervous. Of course she was. So why wasn't her boyfriend helping her out?

'What Dory is trying to say is…' Tyler trailed off, obviously having no idea at all what Dory was trying to say. Which was fair. Lucas wasn't sure Dory had any idea, either.

Lucas rolled his eyes. 'He hasn't been hiding her anywhere,' he said. 'Leave the poor girl be.'

'Well, really, Lucas,' Felicia said. 'We were only trying to get to know her. Find out all the usual things a parent wants to know. Where they met, who her family are, that sort of thing.'

Dory's face turned even paler. Under her dark hair she looked positively deathly.

'Maybe it can wait until dinner?' Tyler suggested, smooth as ever. 'It's been a long drive.'

'Of course, of course!' Suddenly Felicia turned accommodating and understanding. 'You must be exhausted all of you. And the way Lucas takes those corners! Terrifies me.'

'Actually, he was a very considerate driver,' Dory said, giving him a small smile. Lucas felt something inside him start to warm against the chill of Midfield House. Might he actually have an ally here, for once?

Felicia, however, looked disbelieving. 'Really? How unusual.'

'He knows I get travel sick,' Dory added, but Felicia only looked more amazed at the explanation. As if she couldn't imagine her eldest son ever doing such a kindness to a stranger. Or maybe just that it wouldn't occur to her to do the same, Lucas thought.

'Why don't I show you two up to your room,' Felicia said, ushering them towards the staircase. Dory looked around, lip caught between her teeth, and Lucas picked up her bag to hand it to her.

'Oh, leave those,' Patrick said, waving a hand. 'I'll get Duncan to take them up.'

Dory clutched her small case close. 'It's fine, really. It doesn't weigh much.'

Tyler, Lucas couldn't help but notice, left his bag exactly where it was.

'Right.' Felicia looked as though she was searching for her usual aplomb while dealing with this strange woman Tyler had brought home. 'Well, I've put the two of you in the green room, off at the end of the East Wing. You've got your own en-suite, of course. And I thought you might like a bit of privacy.'

Lucas stared at the ceiling and tried very hard not to imagine what his mother thought they were going to do with that privacy.

'That's… great. Thank you.' Dory sounded like she wasn't quite sure what to make of that either.

Tyler, however, frowned. 'The Green Room? Who's in the Blue Room then?'

'The Franklins, tomorrow night, for the party. I promised it to them last year, so they can stay for breakfast, Christmas morning. Now, come on, or you'll never get settled before dinner.'

As the three of them disappeared up the stairs, Dory lugging her case behind her, Lucas told himself that the strange lurch in his stomach was merely a result of being left alone with his father again, not the news that his ex-parents-in-law would be joining them tomorrow.

He didn't bother asking where he was sleeping. Ever since his divorce, he'd been banished to the tiny bedroom above the kitchen, the one Felicia would never use for party guests. Lucas didn't mind. He got more privacy there than even Dory and Tyler would get in the Green Room. And, most importantly, easy access to the leftovers after everyone else had gone to bed.

'Well, then,' Patrick said. 'I don't suppose they'll be very long up there. Why don't we go and get the pre-dinner cocktails started.'

More than anything in the world, Lucas wanted a cold beer, rather than some complicated drink with ingredients he couldn't pronounce. But his father had already disappeared through the doorway into the library, so he followed anyway. He had plenty of time to get settled into his room, after all. His three-day sentence had only just begun.

***

'I do hope you'll find it suitable,' Felicia said, as she flung open the double doors to the Green Room. 'I did worry it might be too small…'

'Oh no,' Dory assured her, staring around the suite. It was bigger than her flat. Possibly bigger than the entire downstairs of her parents' house, actually. 'There's plenty of room for us here.'

'Well, I'll leave the two of you to get settled. Tyler knows where everything is, after all. Come on down for a drink when you've changed, Dory. Tyler, Duncan will bring your bag up shortly.'

'Changed?' Dory asked, as the doors swung shut behind Tyler's mother. 'I have to get changed for dinner?'

Tyler flopped on to the huge double bed that took over the centre of the room. 'It's a thing. They like to dress for dinner.'

Dory looked down at her perfectly chosen, festively evergreen dress. 'I *am* dressed. In a dress, and everything.'

'You are.' Tyler gave her an apologetic smile. 'But could you just…'

'Change.' Dory sighed. 'You owe me cocktails at the airport on my way home for this, you know.'

'I know.'

'And we haven't discussed sleeping arrangements yet.'

'Don't suppose there's any way I can convince you that this bed is big enough for two?'

Dory didn't even bother answering that one as she rummaged through her case, looking for something smart enough for dinner with the Alexanders that wasn't the one posh frock she'd brought for the Christmas Eve party.

In the mirror, she could see Tyler still lying on the bed, eyes closed. 'You better not muss up my covers.'

'You know, the sofa in here is probably very comfortable,' Tyler said. 'And you're shorter. You'd fit on it better.'

Navy dress in hand, Dory turned to face her boss. 'Exactly who is doing whom a favour here?'

'Yeah, yeah. I'm on the floor tonight. I know.' With a groan, Tyler sat up.

Dory held up the dress. 'Will this do?'

Tyler squinted at it. 'Did you bring jewellery?'

'Some.'

'Then yeah, probably.' He paused. 'I really do appreciate you doing this, you know.'

'I know.' Dory dropped to sit on the bed beside him. 'Are we going to tell them about the whole assistant thing? Or just wait and see if Lucas drops us in it?'

'He won't.' Tyler sounded completely confident in that fact. And, surprisingly, so was Dory. She'd only known him for a handful of hours, but she already trusted Tyler's brother. Weird.

'So we don't tell them?'

Tyler hesitated. 'Only if it comes up. Okay?'

'Like if they ask me what I do for a living?'

'Like if they ask you if you're my assistant.'

Ah. That seemed rather less likely, but since it got Dory out of a difficult conversation, she wasn't complaining. They were already lying to his entire family about their relationship, anyway. What was one more little fib?

There was a knock at the door and Tyler yelled, 'Come in!'

A stern-looking man – Duncan, Dory presumed – opened the

door just enough to place Tyler's case inside the room and nod at them both, then he disappeared again.

'Guess we'd better get changed,' Dory said, as Tyler crossed the room to fetch his case. 'Do you want the bathroom or the bedroom?'

'You get changed in here,' Tyler said. 'That way you can fix your make-up in the dressing-table mirror.'

Dory glanced at her reflection. She'd planned on redoing her lipstick, and touching up her powder, of course. But now she just wanted to ask what was wrong with her make-up in the first place?

She sighed at herself in the mirror as Tyler disappeared into the bathroom, then set about removing her make-up, ready to start over.

Apparently impressing the parents was harder than she'd remembered.

Chapter 4

'Martini or a champagne cocktail?' Patrick barely looked up from the drinks cabinet as he asked.

'Beer?' Lucas figured it was worth a try.

'Not before dinner, Lucas,' his mother said from the doorway. 'Mix him a martini, Patrick.'

That, Lucas reflected, was one of the many things he had been positively joyous to leave behind him when he called time on his career as the Alexander Dynasty Heir. On his farm, away from his family, there was no one else to make better choices for him, regardless of what he actually wanted himself.

Lucas decided, there and then, that he was ditching the martini for a beer at the first possible opportunity. A minor rebellion, but it felt important. If a man couldn't pick his own drink at the age of thirty-three, what was the point of it all anyway?

'Tyler and… Dory, was it? All settled in, are they?' Patrick handed Lucas his unwanted martini. Lucas glared at it.

Felicia sighed, that sad, disappointed sigh that Lucas remembered too well from his childhood. The one that said, 'I've done all that I can, and still the world lets me down.' He hated that sigh.

'I hope so. I think Dory is, perhaps, a little… overwhelmed. Not used to… well, you know.' The Alexanders' ridiculous standard in opulence, Lucas assumed she meant.

'What?' Patrick asked, obviously less able to make the mental leap. 'Beds? Indoor plumbing?'

'Patrick,' Felicia said, censoriously, although Lucas was sure she'd been thinking exactly the same thing.

'She's a long way from home at Christmas,' Lucas said, thinking of Dory's homesick Christmas playlist. 'And presumably giving up the holidays with her family to be here, because you insisted that Tyler bring her. I don't think you can blame her for feeling a bit out of place.'

Felicia's eyebrows raised, more in surprise than anything else. 'Why, Lucas, I hadn't realised you'd grown so close to your brother's girlfriend.'

'We just spent two hours in a car together, Mother.'

'And she said she didn't want to be here?' Patrick asked. 'A little rude, don't you think?'

'She didn't say anything of the sort,' Lucas said, wondering how he'd ended up defending her. Except, perhaps, that having escaped the general Alexander effect, he was loathe to let anyone else suffer. 'But she's in a new country, for heaven's sake. It's fairly obvious.'

'To you, maybe,' Felicia said. 'Personally, I expect her plans for the holidays are going exactly as she'd hoped.'

'Meaning?'

'Darling, really. You know what these girls are like.'

So that was it. Felicia had assigned Dory the role of gold-digger, and she'd twist every single thing that happened over the next three days to fit that assumption. Poor Dory.

'I think you're wrong about Dory,' he said. 'And about my drink. I'm going to go see if there's any beer in the kitchen fridge.'

'Not so fast, Lucas.' Patrick, standing in the doorway, gave him a steady look. 'First off, I'm not happy about you talking to your mother that way.'

'What way?' God, it was as if he were sixteen again, getting in trouble for the tone of his voice.

Patrick continued without answering the question. 'And

secondly, I have some other things I want to talk to you about before your brother joins us.'

'In that case, I'm definitely going to need that beer.'

'Duncan!' Felicia snapped and, as if by magic, the butler appeared.

'Yes, Mrs Alexander?'

'Could you please fetch Lucas a beer. In a glass.'

'Of course.' Duncan disappeared as quickly as he'd arrived.

Lucas considered. On the one hand, he'd got his beer. On the other… whatever his father wanted to talk to him about must be more important than drinks decorum. Not a great sign.

Dropping into one of the leather armchairs beside the fire, Lucas placed his still-full martini glass on the nearest side table. Apprehension twisted in his gut. Why couldn't he have just insisted on spending Christmas alone on the farm? He could even have skipped the God-awful Alexander Christmas Eve Party. Next year…

'Regardless of Dory's… suitability,' Patrick started, looking as awkward at the conversation as Lucas felt. 'At least Tyler has brought someone home to meet us. Someone serious. Whereas, as far as we can tell, you haven't dated anyone since…'

'Since Cheryl,' Lucas finished for him, a little confused. This wasn't at all the way he'd expected this conversation to go. 'Well, you know, divorce…' he trailed off, unable to explain to his parents that after what happened with Cheryl it was hard to trust that any woman wouldn't behave exactly as she had, when they realised that this really was who he was these days. He wasn't playing at opting out until he decided it was time to take his rightful place in the Alexander dynasty again. He was done.

It had taken Cheryl six months after the accident to realise that. And when she had… she'd packed and left the next day. And then she'd taken him for everything she could get in the divorce.

His mother came and perched on the arm of his chair, looking suddenly intent and almost frighteningly maternal. Lucas tried not to flinch as she leant in to pat his shoulder. 'You can't let it knock you back like this, Lucas. It's time for you to get back in the game.'

'The… dating game?' Lucas's voice squeaked a little as he spoke the words. Duncan, who'd finally reappeared with his beer, raised his eyebrows a little at the sound. Lucas suspected he was going to get mocked later, when he got together with the butler and Freya, the maid, for poker, as per their private tradition.

'The game of life, if you will.' Patrick took the glass and handed the drink to Lucas, who took a quick, desperate gulp.

Then his father's words registered. Suddenly, everything made a lot more sense. 'This isn't just an intervention in my love life, is it?'

'Of course not.' Felicia slipped off the arm of the chair and stood by her husband. 'There are far more important things at stake than who you bring home to meet the family.'

'Like the family business,' Patrick said.

Lucas shook his head. 'I've told you before. I'm happy where I am, doing what I'm doing. And Tyler wants to be CEO. We're both happy with how things are.'

'It's not all about being happy, though, is it,' Felicia said, and Lucas felt a sudden pang of sadness for his parents.

It didn't last long, though.

'You need to think about your legacy,' Patrick said. 'About your contribution to the family, and its place in this world. In society, in business. You are part of something important. You were born into privilege, and that has its obligations.'

Lucas thought about Henry, dead at thirty-one because of his obligations to family and legacy. Because he thought it meant living up to the illusion of having everything, doing everything better, being everything that someone else wanted to be. That wouldn't happen to him.

'Not anymore, I don't. I gave back the place on the board, my position. I don't owe anyone anything any longer.'

'That's not how it works.' Felicia's voice was stern, unwavering.

Lucas drained the rest of his beer. 'It is now.' Getting to his feet, he headed for the door. 'Now, if you'll excuse me, I'm going to see if Duncan's hiding any more of this in the fridge before I get changed for dinner.'

'This conversation isn't over,' Felicia said, following him.

'Yes.' Lucas turned to her, quick enough that she had to take a step back. 'It is.' Then, he made his way to the kitchen. Clearly this weekend was going to need a lot of beer. He just hoped that Duncan had stocked up.

***

'Am I presentable?' Dory asked, giving Tyler a little twirl as he came out of the bathroom, decked out in a shirt, tie and jacket.

He flashed her a smile. 'Ravishing.'

She didn't feel it. In fact, she felt kind of frumpy, but she had a feeling that the pearls and boring dress were probably what the Alexanders were looking for in Tyler's girlfriend, anyway. Silently, she thanked the last-minute impulse that had made her pack them.

'Guess we'd better go face the music, then,' she said.

Tyler took her arm. 'Don't worry. They'll love you.'

Dory couldn't help the burst of laughter that came out at that. 'Tyler, they're going to hate me. They were always going to hate me. There is pretty much nothing I can do to change that, and the only thing that could make it worse is if they found out I'm actually your assistant.'

'Good job you're not actually dating me then, huh?'

Dory shuddered. 'A very good job.' Just the thought of a future of Christmases spent at Midfield House made her feel faintly sick.

'They're not so bad, you know,' Tyler said, more seriously.

'To you, no,' Dory replied. 'But I don't belong here, and they know it. That's all.'

Tyler opened the door. 'Come on. At least the food should make up for everything else.'

'And the wine?'

'The wine, I promise you, will be superb.'

It was, too. Dory took a sip, and reminded herself to go slow with it. The last thing they needed was her getting tipsy and saying something she shouldn't.

'So, Dory, I trust you've recovered from your motion sickness?' Felicia looked pointedly at Dory's empty plate and she realised, too late, that everyone apart from Lucas was still only halfway through their starters.

'I'm feeling much better, thank you,' she said, giving Tyler's mother a tight smile. She took another tiny sip of her wine. Felicia's frown deepened, and Dory thought, *Screw it*, and took a bigger gulp. As she put the glass down, Lucas reached across the table and topped up her wine. The smile she gave him, at least, was genuine. Anyone who took care of her wine needs without judgement was definitely on her side.

As the maid cleared their starter plates, Patrick leant back in his seat at the head of the table. Feeling his eyes on her, Dory looked up. Tyler's father made her a little uncomfortable, she had to admit. Maybe it was just that while Felicia's disdain was evident from a mile away, Patrick tried to exude more of a friendly vibe – but she still got the feeling he was just waiting for her to trip up.

'So, Dory,' he said, lifting his own wine glass. 'Where would you be spending Christmas this year if my son hadn't brought you home to share the season with us?'

A wave of homesickness hit Dory in the chest. Except she wouldn't have been at home, would she? And Tyler's girlfriend certainly wouldn't have been abandoning Manhattan for Liverpool. 'Oh, I'd still be in New York,' she said, hoping her bright smile didn't look as fake as it felt. 'Probably spending the day with my girlfriends, I suppose. Drinking champagne and eating truffles.' Or, in reality, shivering under her duvet with a cup of tea and a turkey ready-meal for one, watching the Doctor Who Christmas Special and listening to Cliff Richard.

Across the table, Lucas gave her a disbelieving look. Apparently he thought her taste in Christmas music had given him some sort of insight into her real festive plans. Damn. She was going to have to be careful with Lucas.

'Not with your family?' Felicia asked, and Dory tried to quickly figure out exactly what she was being disapproved of for now. Was it for not spending Christmas with her family? Or for having a family who didn't demand she spend the holidays with them or that she didn't want to be with over the festive season? *If only they knew the truth…*

'I'm going home to visit over New Year,' Dory explained, as the maid brought their main courses out. Some sort of fancy duck dish with a berry sauce. It smelled wonderful. 'It worked out better with my work commitments, and I can stay longer then.' The total truth. She intended to make sure Tyler honoured his promise to give her a full two weeks off with her family, starting with her flight out on the 27th December. It was only when she saw Lucas wince across the table that she realised what she'd done.

'So, you work, then?' Felicia asked. Dory took a large bite of duck to help resist the urge to reply that, yes, of course she worked! Almost everybody did, these days. Except, of course, in Felicia Alexander's world. 'What is it that you do?'

Dory glanced at Tyler before she answered. *Lie*, he mouthed. Dory took a breath. She could do that. She'd been lying to her parents about it for six months, after all.

'I'm in PR,' she said, and watched Lucas's eyebrows rise. 'I was brought over from the UK to work on a number of very high-profile campaigns.' That much was true, anyway. When she'd told her boss that her fiancé was moving to New York and wanted her to go with him, Melanie had been thrilled. Apparently she'd been trying to decide between Dory and two of her colleagues to go on a secondment over at the Manhattan office of their company anyway. Dory had been her first choice, but she'd been uncertain whether she'd want to go, having just got engaged. This way, Dory could make her mark in the States and then, hopefully, secure a permanent role over there once the secondment was up. In one fell swoop, Dory had fixed Melanie's problem and changed her whole life.

Of course, neither of them could have predicted that, by the time the three-month secondment ended, the company would have restructured and there wouldn't be a job left for Dory, or Melanie, in the US or UK offices.

'That sounds very interesting,' Patrick said, between mouthfuls, although he didn't sound particularly interested. 'We have an excellent PR team at the Alexander Corporation, you know.'

'So I understand,' Dory said. In fact, she knew first-hand. She knew exactly how much effort went into making sure that Tyler appeared at the right events, with the right person, doing the right things.

She wondered how much the PR team would scream if they knew what she and Tyler were doing this weekend. Who would cry, if and when, they found out.

'You should see if Tyler can get you a job there,' Lucas said, and Dory narrowed her eyes at his smirk. Wasn't he supposed to be on her side?

'Oh, I don't think that would be very appropriate,' Felicia said, which Dory interpreted as meaning 'she'll be so much harder to get rid of then.' 'After all, what would the press make of Tyler dating a colleague?'

Tyler choked on his wine.

'This duck is delicious, Mrs Alexander,' Dory said, in a desperate attempt to change the subject.

'Well, thank you, Dory. How nice of you to say.' She made it sound as if she'd been slaving over a hot stove all afternoon cooking it, when everyone around the table knew full well that their chef was responsible. Dory supposed it was one of those pretensions the rich liked to keep up. 'I can see you're certainly enjoying it.'

Dory paused, forkful of meat and berries halfway to her mouth. And then she ate it anyway, because what was there to say to that, really? At least they weren't talking about her working for Tyler any longer.

It was only for three days. She could endure any amount of rudeness and pretension for three days, right? And at the end of it, she'd be home where she belonged for two whole weeks.

Dory looked down at her plate, wishing she could ask for seconds. But that would just give Felicia more ammunition against her. And for the next three days, she needed to be, if not the perfect girlfriend, at least a believable one.

Just three days. Then she would be eating every leftover mince pie in Liverpool.

***

Lucas studied Dory as the others finished up their main courses. So far, she seemed to be holding up under his mother's passive-aggressive condescension. Good for her. Of course, she'd probably be dealing with it better if her boyfriend helped out...

He let his gaze drift over to his brother, sitting next to Dory. For all the attention he was paying her, he could be at an entirely separate dinner. The only time he'd looked up at her was when their mother had asked what Dory did for a living. And then, Lucas had seen Dory check with Tyler before answering. Had he told her to lie? Probably.

Not for the first time, Lucas wished he wasn't in on this secret. All three of them knew that it was a potential media disaster. The press were still trying to find out who the woman in the photos was. Suddenly Lucas was glad he'd driven them north. Someone would have got a photo on the train and it would have been all over the Internet in seconds.

Even without that, what were the chances of their parents not figuring it out? Lucas didn't like to weigh them up. They weren't stupid people. All it would take would be one slip from Dory, or Tyler, hell even himself, and the rest of the Christmas holiday

44

would be spent in crisis meetings with the PR team. Nobody's idea of a dream weekend.

But still, Lucas couldn't help but wonder just how long Tyler intended to keep up this charade. If he and Dory were serious – and the fact he'd actually brought her home for Christmas, even if it was only because Felicia had nagged, suggested that they were – then eventually the truth would have to come out. Even if they had plans for her to leave her job, maybe even move into the PR department like Patrick had suggested, someone would put it together eventually. Hopefully far enough down the line for no one to really care. After all, breaking the story that the CEO of the Alexander Corporation was actively sleeping with his assistant, potentially on company time, was one thing. Discovering, a couple of years down the line, that they'd actually got together while she was working as his assistant, then she'd moved on so they could pursue a relationship, was something entirely different.

Lucas shook his head. He was thinking like a businessman again. Like the Alexander family heir. Like all those things he'd given up. What did he care what the papers said? Or the board, for that matter? They weren't part of his life anymore.

But Dory might be. Tyler had been talking marriage in the car. Hypothetical marriage, of course, and disturbingly involving his ex-wife in the conversation, but still. He'd never heard his brother even mention himself and marriage in the same sentence before. Was he planning on making Dory a more permanent fixture in all their lives?

Across the table, she ducked her head over her empty plate, as Felicia started recounting the guest list for their traditional Christmas Eve party. Designed, no doubt, to intimidate Dory and make her nervous. Every year, they invited 'everyone who is anyone, darling,' in upstate New York, and every year, to Lucas's ongoing amazement, they all came. Didn't they have anything better to do with their holidays? Or did they just fear what might happen if they skipped it? Lucas had never been sure, but he suspected the wrath of Felicia might have a lot to do with it.

'I do hope Tyler warned you about our little get together in time for you to arrange an appropriate dress, Dory,' Felicia said.

Dory looked up, a flash of a smile on her painted red lips. She was almost a Christmas decoration herself, Lucas thought.

'I'm certain I have something suitable in my bag,' Dory said.

'Are you sure?' Felicia's concern was completely feigned, Lucas knew. 'I know how hard it can be when you're not used to this sort of society.' Another lie. Felicia Alexander had never known anything *but* this sort of society.

Lucas looked over at his brother. Was Tyler really just going to sit there while their mother spoke to his girlfriend this way? He frowned. Tyler didn't even seem to be paying attention to the conversation. Instead, he stared down at his lap… Lucas narrowed his eyes. Was Tyler on his phone at the dinner table? Checking his email, no doubt, or the share price.

Not paying attention to the beautiful woman he'd brought into the lions' den.

'I'm sure Dory knows her wardrobe best, Mother,' Lucas said. Then he spotted Freya, the maid, in the doorway. 'Fantastic. Dessert.'

Dory looked up too, obviously eager, but Felicia got there first.

'Thank you, Freya, but I won't be having dessert tonight.' She gave Dory a flat smile. 'And I'm sure Dory feels the same. After all, we have dresses to fit into!'

Anger bubbled up in Lucas's gut as he watched Dory's smile stiffen. For a moment, he thought that she might tell Felicia where to stick her dresses, but she obviously swallowed it down. 'Good idea, Felicia,' was all she said.

Freya took the unwanted plates back to the kitchen. Lucas wondered if they'd still be in the fridge later. He could smuggle one up to Dory's room for her… except he couldn't. Because she'd be in bed with his brother. His idiot, distracted, undeserving brother.

He really should try harder to remember that.

Tearing his eyes away from Dory, who was staring at the oblivious Tyler's chocolate pistachio gateau, Lucas focused on his own dessert. In and out. That was the plan. He wasn't going to get involved. Not with his family's issues, not with the business, and not, most definitely not, with Dory and Tyler's relationship. In and out. In three days he'd be back on his farm, checking in at the restaurant, working on his own dreams, and he could forget about the obligations and expectations of the Alexander name for another year.

Just three more days until he got his real life back.

***

Relief washed over Dory as the maid cleared the last of the dessert plates and Felicia stood, ready to leave the room. Dory followed suit, and it wasn't until she'd tucked her chair back under the table that a truly horrible thought occurred to her. What if this was that thing she'd read about it books – the ladies retiring to another room to do cross-stitch or something while the guys drank brandy? She did not want to be left alone with Felicia. She'd have sent Dory for an extreme makeover before Tyler had even had his first sip.

'Well, I need to go check through some final party prep with Freya,' Felicia said. Dory hoped her answering sigh of relief wasn't too obvious. 'So I'll see you all in the morning.'

'And I need to…' Dory tried to think of something that wasn't 'get the hell out of here, quickly.' 'Get some sleep,' she finished. 'So I'm going to head up to bed.'

She gave Tyler a meaningful look, one that she hoped he interpreted as 'give me ten minutes to get changed, then come up to bed so they think we're crazy about each other,' but she suspected he'd probably take as 'stay and enjoy some brandy with your father and brother!' He'd never been all that good at the secret signals thing. It had caused problems a couple of times at important charity events, usually when Tyler hadn't read the briefing documents she'd put together for him beforehand.

Still, at least that meant she could get some quiet alone time, without anyone suggesting that she was so fat and uncultured that she'd be a positive embarrassment at the traditional Alexander Family Christmas Eve party.

Upstairs, the Green Room felt positively serene compared to sitting around the dining table. Letting the door fall closed behind her, Dory leant back against it, just enjoying breathing without criticism.

God, I want some of that chocolate cake.

Too late now, though. Felicia had pretty clearly closed the cake avenue to her. With a sigh, Dory pushed up from the door and grabbed her pyjamas from the pillow. On the vague off-chance that Tyler had picked up the correct signals, she wanted to be changed and in bed by the time he came up for the night. Just in case he forgot about their sofa deal.

A while later, face scrubbed of make-up, pyjamas on and curled up on the bed, Dory finished her book and tossed her e-reader aside. Clearly, Tyler hadn't understood the meaningful look. Again.

And she still really wanted cake.

She should get some sleep.

Snuggling down under the absurdly comfortable duvet, Dory closed her eyes. Pointed her toes and stretched her legs. Pulled her arms out and put them on top of the duvet. Tucked them back in again.

Opened her eyes and sighed. Then she sat up.

Felicia be damned. She was getting cake.

Chapter 5

'Brandy, boys?' Patrick already had the bottle in his hand and three glasses set out on the table, so Lucas assumed this was a rhetorical question. Still, his father's distraction with the perfect quantity of ice per glass gave him the opportunity he needed to talk to Tyler.

'Aren't you going to go and check on Dory?' He was not getting involved, Lucas told himself. He was just… nudging Tyler into decent human behaviour. Too much time as an Alexander tended to strip people of that, and Lucas liked to think that there was still a glimmer of hope for his brother.

'Dory? Why?' Tyler placed his phone screen-down on the table. 'She's probably asleep by now.'

'After that dinner? I doubt it.'

Tyler's brow crinkled up. 'What was wrong with dinner? She said she was feeling better after the car ride, right?'

Was his brother really that obtuse? Or had he just not been paying attention that evening? Lucas watched as Tyler picked up his phone again, tapping at the screen.

'How about a cigar?' Patrick asked. 'I've got some special ones put aside in the study. I'll fetch them. One moment.' He strolled out of the room towards the other end of the hall.

Lucas grabbed the brandy closest to him and pushed it across to Tyler, then selected another glass for himself. 'So. When are you going to tell them?'

'Tell them what?'

'The truth about Dory.'

Tyler's gaze jerked up from the phone screen. 'What do you mean?'

'That she's your assistant. Remember?'

'Oh. That.' Tyler's head dipped back down and his fingers started moving over the screen again. 'Hopefully never.'

'So you'll… what? Shift her to the PR department before anyone finds out?'

'Something like that, yeah.'

Lucas watched him for a moment. This was not his business. He did not care what Tyler did about Dory. Hell, he'd deserve it if she walked out on him for being a stupid, inattentive bastard.

Except… Lucas couldn't help remembering the way Dory had bossed Tyler around at the office. The way she'd stood her ground against him. How she'd seemed like she might actually be a match for his stubbornness and confidence – at least until she came up against Felicia Alexander.

Nobody deserved that. Especially not Dory.

'And you've… spoken to Dory about the plan?'

Sighing, Tyler put his phone down again. 'Look, don't worry about it, okay? Dory knows the score.'

Somehow, that totally failed to make Lucas feel any better at all.

Taking a gulp of his brandy, Lucas pushed the glass across the table and got to his feet. 'Okay, I know I'm not the world's best advisor on women. And quite honestly, I really don't want to get involved in your relationship, or the craziness that will follow if our mother figures out what's actually going on here. But if you have any sense at all, you'll go up to your room now and apologise to Dory for our parents.' Piece said, he made his way to the door, until one final thought made him pause. 'And Tyler, I'd take cake.'

Tyler's confused expression suggested that his advice was destined to be ignored, but somehow Lucas felt a little lighter, anyway. He'd done his bit. Now he could go to bed without feeling guilty, and tomorrow it was back to the plan. In and out and back to his real life. Easy.

'She'll probably be asleep anyway,' Tyler said. 'I can talk to her in the morning. Besides, I want one of Dad's cigars.'

Lucas sighed. 'I'll see you in the morning.' Assuming Dory didn't smother Tyler in his sleep through sheer frustration.

***

No one had offered her a tour of Midfield House, so finding the kitchens was a bit hit and miss. Wincing as her bare toes hit the cold tiles of the back hallway, Dory figured she had to at least be getting close. She'd skirted the main hall, ducking behind a pillar as Patrick walked past with a box of cigars. Then, using a process of elimination, she darted through the small doorway to the back hallway that screamed 'servants' quarters.'

Then she saw it. The Holy Grail. The wide, clear, wooden surfaces, the oversized range cooker, the scrubbed kitchen table. And there, in the corner, the huge, American-style refrigerator. Somewhere in there, surely, there had to be cake.

Skipping over the icy floor tiles, Dory made her way to the fridge, yanking the door open and staring inside.

No cake.

Salad, fruit, cold meats and cheeses… but absolutely no cake.

Where the hell was the cake?

The fridge door didn't even slam very satisfyingly. Dory clunked her head against the cool surface and thought hard. If she were a maid in this hateful house, where would she hide leftover cake?

'It's in the pantry fridge.'

Dory's heart bounced up to her throat at the words, and she spun round so fast her foot slipped on the tiles. Grabbing the counter to keep herself upright, she stared at Tyler's brother with wide eyes.

51

'I'm sorry, I was just looking for—'

'Cake,' Lucas finished for her. 'Like I say, Freya always keeps the desserts in the other fridge. In the pantry.'

Biting her lip, Dory shrugged. 'You caught me. I like dessert.'

'I could tell,' Lucas said. 'I saw your eyes widen when Freya brought it in earlier.'

'It did look amazing.'

'And your face fall when my mother cake-blocked you.'

'I'm sure she had my best interests at heart,' Dory lied. Felicia Alexander might be an utter snake, but she was still Lucas's mother. Men didn't tend to take too kindly to other women criticising their mothers, and the last thing she needed was Lucas reporting back to the family that Dory was badmouthing them behind their backs.

But to her surprise, Lucas laughed and said, 'Oh, I doubt it. Usually the only interests she has at heart – or anywhere – are her own.'

'Does that mean you're not going to tell her if I eat the leftover cake?' Dory asked.

Lucas's smile turned sly. 'Well now, that depends.'

'On what?'

'On whether you're willing to share.'

Dory grinned. 'I think I might be persuaded. Want to grab the cake?' She stared around the massive kitchen. 'I'll start hunting the drawers for forks.'

Lucas was already halfway across the room, heading for a plain wood door Dory hadn't even spotted before. The pantry, she supposed. Just as well Lucas had happened along; she'd never have found the cake there.

'Three drawers to the left of the sink,' he called back.

Dory counted handles along from the sink and found, lo and behold, a whole drawer full of forks. Pastry forks, cake forks, smaller forks for starters, and full-sized dining forks. Mind slightly boggled, she pulled open the next drawer. Knives. Lots of knives. Fish knives, steak knives, knives for every possible conceivable occasion. At that point, she couldn't leave the last drawer unopened. Inside, neatly ordered into sections, were spoons varying in size from tiny coffee spoons, all the way up to serving spoons, via a number of different sizes she couldn't even have guessed names or uses for.

'You casing the silver?' Dory jumped at Lucas's words. 'Because I'll give you a tip. The really expensive stuff is in the chest in the main hall.'

Dory slammed the drawers shut, keeping only the two cake forks she'd picked out in the first place. 'Just wondering who really needs that much cutlery.' She shook her head as she joined him at the table. He hadn't bothered with separate plates, just brought the chocolate and pistachio gateau on the serving plate Freya had left it on. 'It's a different world.'

'You're telling me,' Lucas said, taking the fork she offered him. 'I grew up here, and it still baffles me. Especially since I think I might be the only family member who knows where anything is in this kitchen.'

'Yeah, I was kinda surprised by that.' Dory cut off the tiniest sliver of chocolate cake with the edge of her fork. She wanted to savour this…

'My room is just upstairs,' Lucas explained. 'And I like to save the family dining for special occasions. Which means if I want to eat the rest of the time, I had to figure out where things are.' He shrugged. 'Besides, Duncan and Freya are more fun to hang out with, anyway. We usually play poker in the evenings, when I'm here, but apparently party prep has taken over tonight.'

Tilting her head, Dory considered Tyler's older brother. From his short cropped hair, lighter than Tyler's messy style, to the stubble that was just a millimetre too long to be truly designer, he didn't look like an Alexander. Didn't embrace the name and all it brought with it, the way Tyler did. And here, now, she wanted to ask why.

'You're not comfortable here, are you?' she said, then winced. Too blunt, again, Dory. She could almost hear her father whispering 'a little subtlety, maybe?' in her ear. 'Sorry. I just mean…'

'That I'd obviously rather be somewhere else?' Lucas finished for her. 'It's okay; you're right.'

'So, where would you rather be?'

'Honestly? Pretty much anywhere.' He sighed. 'But right now, given the choice, I'd be home on my farm.'

Dory blinked. 'You own a *farm?*'

'Kinda. But probably not the sort you're thinking of.'

'Pigs? Sheep? That kind of thing?'

'Well… yeah. But to be honest, I'm not that involved with the actually farming side of things. I rent out the land to local farmers, mostly.'

'So… what *do* you do, then?'

'Enjoy the peace and quiet?' Dory raised her eyebrows at him, and he sighed. 'Yeah, you're not going to accept that answer, are you?'

'Somehow I can't imagine you sitting in a rocking chair on a porch somewhere, while other people do all the fun stuff.'

'Fair enough.' He dropped his cake fork onto the plate. There wasn't much cake left now, anyway. 'How much do you know about me?'

Dory shrugged. 'Only what it says in your Wikipedia entry.'

'I have a…' He shook his head. 'Never mind. I'm sure it told you that I kinda… dropped out of society a couple of years ago.'

'When you got divorced,' Dory said, then bit her lip. 'Sorry about that.'

'Don't be,' Lucas said, absently. 'Besides, that's the wrong way round. Cheryl left me because I wasn't living the life she married me for anymore.'

'Why not?' Dory asked, curious. 'I mean, most people would kill for this sort of existence.'

'Would you?'

'Well… no. But lots of people.'

'Yeah, well, not me either.'

'But you did,' Dory said. 'You ran the company before Tyler

took it over.'

'And I ran it damn well. But then…' Lucas paused, as if trying to find the words. 'You know how, sometimes, something happens that changes your whole life. The whole way you see the world.'

'I guess,' Dory said. Losing her job, she supposed. Or agreeing to move to New York. Or the day she came home to find Ewen in bed with the hot, blonde, Manhattan socialite. That was a big one.

'There was an accident.' Lucas looked down at his empty hands. 'My best friend… he died. He was showing off, living the high life, fooling around on his speedboat to impress his fiancée. Except it went wrong. I was in hospital for weeks, unconscious for most of it. And when I woke up, he was gone.'

Dory's heart clenched at the matter-of-fact way he told the story. However hard he tried to sound unemotional about it, the tension in his jaw, the way his fingers flexed, told her otherwise. 'That's… God, Lucas, that's awful.' Without thinking, she reached across and grabbed his hand, holding those tight, tense fingers in hers.

Lucas looked up, giving her a half smile. 'Yeah. It was. Tyler never told you about this?'

Dory shook her head. 'Tyler doesn't really talk about… well, you.'

'The black sheep, huh?'

'Pretty much.'

He squeezed her fingers, then let go of her hand. 'Well, at least it was my choice. I took my money – not the business's money, or the family's, just what I'd earned myself over the last however many years – and I left. I bought my farm, holed up there for a while. And then, well, I got bored.'

'Thought as much.' Dory took one last mouthful of cake from the plate. 'So, back to my original question. What do you do now?'

Lucas shrugged and picked up his fork again. 'I wanted to do something new, but using what I'd learnt in the family business. Something I could get in on the ground floor of, not be stuck up in some office somewhere. So I set up my own restaurant, in one of the old barns at the edge of the farm, closest to the road into the nearest town.'

'I'm guessing this restaurant is not another Alexander's.'

'No.' Lucas laughed. 'My father would hate it. It's all organic, local food on the menu, for locals to eat. We grow or rear most of it on my farm.'

'Sounds wonderful.' And totally unlike the corporate, establishment Alexander Corporation and its identikit chain restaurants.

'We'll see. It's still just starting out. I guess I was just looking for something that's mine. That I can build up myself.'

Dory thought about how she'd followed Ewen across an ocean, only to be cut adrift. And now she was at Tyler's beck and call instead. 'I can understand that.'

'Yeah,' Lucas said, staring at her, an odd look in his eye. 'Somehow, I thought you might.'

***

Lucas tore his gaze away from Dory, from the way her lips wrapped around that last mouthful of chocolate cake, and how her shoulders wriggled under her strappy pyjama top at the taste. It took considerably more effort than it should. Was that why he couldn't shake the feeling he was doing something wrong? In reality, all he'd done was make polite conversation with a woman who might one day be his sister-in-law. Perfectly reasonable.

Except it hadn't all been polite. And a lot of it had been things he hadn't spoken about to anyone else since Cheryl left. Least of all his actual family, mostly because they simply weren't prepared to listen.

Dory listened. Dory not only showed interest in what he had to say but… she seemed to care about it, too. On less than twelve hours' acquaintance. A hell of a better record than his parents or brother had in this matter.

But she was Tyler's. So a good listener was all she could ever be to him, however well they'd bonded over cake.

Still… at least he should return the favour.

Clearing his throat, Lucas speared a few cake crumbs and some icing with his fork. 'So, what about you? What would you really be doing for Christmas if you weren't here? And not the story you told my mother at dinner. Where would you want to be?'

'Ideally?' Dory asked. 'I'd be at home in Liverpool, drinking mulled wine and eating mince pies. Playing board games with my family. Watching Doctor Who on Christmas Day. Opening our stockings. That sort of thing.'

'Sounds nice.' His Christmases had never been like that, even as a child. There were always guests – usually people his parents were trying to impress – and itchy, formal outfits to be worn. 'And instead, you're here.'

'Instead, I'm here,' Dory agreed.

'You must really love my brother,' Lucas joked, but Dory didn't laugh. In fact, she looked positively uncomfortable. 'Still, you survived your first Alexander family dinner. Think you can make it through the next few days without losing your mind?'

The face she pulled suggested that Dory wasn't entirely sure she could. 'I'm just focusing on getting to go home for two whole weeks after this.'

He wasn't surprised that she'd rather be with her own family, whatever Felicia's assumptions. 'Think Tyler will be able to cope without you for that long?'

'He'll have to,' Dory said, face stubborn. 'That was the deal.'

'Deal?'

The colour faded from Dory's cheeks, as if she'd said something she hadn't meant to. 'Um, yeah. Well, I mean, he promised that if I came and spent Christmas with his family, he'd give me a couple of weeks off to visit mine over New Year. Not that I didn't want to be with him for Christmas, or anything. Or here. Um…'

'I get it, Dory,' Lucas said, deciding the only decent thing was to put her out of her misery. 'It's okay to want to be with your own family for the holidays. Especially when the other option is my family.'

She gave him a faint smile, but nothing like the way she'd beamed at him when he'd placed the chocolate cake on the table. She looked… scared, almost. Lucas couldn't shake the feeling that he'd missed something, somewhere. Something important. His mind flicked back over every conversation he'd had with Dory, through cake and cutlery and Christmas music until it reached… the phone call. His call to Tyler's office.

He frowned at the memory. 'You know, I was thinking. You never said anything about you and Tyler when I called that day.'

'Oh. Well. It wasn't really… I mean, I didn't know I would be coming for Christmas until later. Until your mother demanded that Tyler bring the woman in the photos home to meet them. You know?'

She was talking too fast, too sure, and her fingers kept twirling the fork around and around. He was definitely missing something here.

'But you knew it was you in the photos,' he pressed. 'And you didn't say anything.'

'Well, yeah, sure. But it was kind of a delicate situation, right? I mean, I hadn't even seen them until you called. And Tyler didn't want people to know about us, I guess.'

Dory knows the score. That was what Tyler had said. But Lucas was starting to suspect that 'score' wasn't what he'd imagined it to be.

'That makes sense,' he said, because it did. Even if he was almost certain it wasn't the whole truth. 'But I'm kind of surprised. I'd have thought, given everything… Well, I'd have expected him to be a little more protective of you this weekend. Or at least more attentive.'

'You mean, protect me from your mother?' Her hands finally stopped moving, dropping the fork to the wood of the table. 'Well, you know Tyler,' she said, with a small smile. 'He probably doesn't even realise what she's doing.'

'Maybe not,' Lucas conceded.

'Is she like this with every woman you guys bring home?' Dory asked.

Lucas thought back to his conversation with Tyler in the car. 'Not every woman,' he admitted.

'Just me, then,' Dory said. 'It's the accent, isn't it?'

'I like the accent.'

That earned him a real, wide smile. 'You do? Good.'

For a long moment, they just looked at each other, and Lucas wondered how he'd got here, sitting in the kitchen with his brother's girlfriend, desperately trying to think of something more to say, anything to keep her there with him. To stop her going to bed with Tyler.

But he couldn't. He had to let her go. Whatever his suspicions and hopes, he had to let Dory go for tonight.

'I'd better go to bed,' she said. Was that reluctance he heard in her voice? Or was that just wishful thinking? 'Tyler will be wondering where I am.'

He nodded. 'Good night, then. You'd better rest up for more family fun tomorrow.'

'Can't wait!' Dory pushed her chair back and padded to the door, giving him an excellent view of her faded pyjama bottoms curving over her ass. 'Night, Lucas. Sleep tight.'

He nodded, but he knew he wouldn't. Not least because, before he could think about sleep, he had some photos to look at. And some suspicions to resolve.

Chapter 6

Tyler still hadn't made it back to their room by the time Dory, full of cake and apprehension, finally fell into bed. She spared a brief thought for where he might have disappeared to, but mostly she was just grateful for the solitude. She needed to think.

She shouldn't have got so chatty with Lucas. But he'd started sharing about his life, and why he'd pulled away from the Alexander family, and it just seemed natural to let him see a bit of her life too. Even if it wasn't an entirely truthful picture.

But Lucas wasn't stupid. The questions he'd been asking... he had suspicions, she was sure. And she was a lousy liar. If he pressed her any further, she'd cave, she knew she would.

And would that be such a bad thing? Dory tried to mentally shush the devil on her shoulder, but she was a persuasive little creature. In her head, she sounded just like her little sister Molly...

If Lucas found out the truth – that she and Tyler weren't really dating – what would it change? He already knew she was his assistant. What was one more little secret between friends? Especially since Lucas seemed more of a friend to her in this hostile environment than her fake boyfriend did. If Lucas was in on the whole masquerade, he could help her, maybe. Somehow.

She sighed and turned on to her side, burrowing deeper into the duvet. She was making excuses for herself. The truth was, if

Lucas knew she wasn't really dating Tyler, maybe he'd stop holding himself back.

Dory might not have the best track record with men, but she knew enough to know when a guy was interested. She'd seen Lucas's eyes linger on the neckline of her camisole top – and seen him yank his gaze away again. She'd felt the connection in the moments of silence, known when he said more than he meant to just because he couldn't help himself.

She knew that, in other circumstances, he might make a move. Or she might. Not that night, maybe, but one night, and soon.

But not if he thought she was dating his brother.

The problem was, of course, that even if she told him the truth, she couldn't do anything about the attraction between them. She was there with Tyler, that was the deal. And if somebody stumbled across her and Lucas… well, the jig would be up and her ticket home was sure to be cancelled.

Flipping on to her back, she stared up at the ceiling again. There was only one thing for it – she just had to wait it out. Eventually, Tyler would have to come clean about who the woman in the photos really was. Or, even if he didn't, he'd fake break-up with her, or vice versa, and she'd be free of all this. And maybe then, just maybe, she could call Lucas up and ask if he had a table free at that restaurant of his…

When she finally dozed off, imagining a farmhouse kitchen and another chocolate cake, Tyler still hadn't come to bed.

He was there when she woke up the next morning, though, passed out on the sofa with a blanket tugged over his t-shirt and a bare, hairy calf sticking out the end. Dory stared down at him, wondering how on earth he'd managed to sleep in such an uncomfortable position. His arm lolled off the edge of the sofa, his phone on the floor just below. It must have slipped out of his fingers when he dropped off. Knowing he was bound to stand on it when he woke up – and then blame her for it somehow – Dory picked it up to put on the table. As she did, the screen lit up, and she couldn't help but read the notifications. Three missed calls and eight text messages. All from one person – someone Tyler had stored in his phone as 'Angel.'

Was that a name or an endearment, Dory wondered? Not that it mattered. It had to be the woman in the photos, right? And Dory had no interest in finding out her identity until *after* her trip home. No questions. That was Tyler's rule.

Placing the phone securely on the coffee table, she headed for the shower, only to freeze when the phone started ringing.

Holding her breath, Dory stood in the middle of the room, waiting for Tyler to wake up and answer it. But the only sign that Tyler was even still alive was the loud snore he gave out as he turned over.

She should ignore it. It wasn't any of her business. Except… clearly this woman was going to keep ringing. And Dory's restraint only went so far…

With a muttered curse, she spun round and grabbed the phone again. *Angel,* the screen read, unsurprisingly. Dory pressed answer.

'Hello? Tyler Alexander's phone. Can I help you?' she asked, in her best bubbly assistant voice.

There was a long pause on the other end. Then, finally, a woman said, 'Is Tyler there?'

'I'm afraid he's… indisposed right now. I'm his assistant, Dory. Can I take a message.'

'Yes. No.' The woman sighed. 'I guess… just ask him to call Cheryl, yeah?'

Cheryl. Not Angel. So now she had a name, and Dory really wished she didn't. *Cheryl left me because I wasn't living the life she married me for anymore.* Lucas's words from the night before echoed around her head.

'Of course. I'll tell him,' she said, mind reeling, but Cheryl had already hung up.

Tyler, what the hell are you doing?

Lucas was already at the dining table when Dory walked in for breakfast. Had already been there a while, in fact, even though he could have done with another hour in bed. He hadn't wanted to miss her.

His father sat at one end of the table, engrossed in the paper. Felicia was nowhere to be seen, although she could certainly be heard.

'What do you mean it *hasn't been delivered?*' Felicia reached an almost shriek on the last few words, and Dory froze in the doorway.

Lucas raised an eyebrow at her and, for a moment, she stared back, before she shook her head and slipped into the chair she'd been sitting in for dinner the night before. Had she spent the night berating herself for giving away too much to him? Probably. Dory seemed the sort to overthink things. Not that it mattered, at this point. *Too late now, sweetheart.*

'What's going on?' she asked across the table, voice low, presumably so she didn't interrupt Felicia's high-pitched rant at poor Freya.

'Looks like the Christmas tree hasn't turned up,' he explained, helping himself to more eggs. 'Mother always wants to leave it until the last minute so it looks perfect for the party.'

'I didn't expect to see you for breakfast.' Dory glanced at him under her lashes as she reached for the coffee pot.

'I bumped into Tyler late last night,' Lucas explained. 'He didn't look as if he was likely to be up early this morning, so I figured you might need some moral support.'

'That was nice of you,' Dory said, surprised.

Lucas shrugged. 'Just another two days to go,' he said. 'I figure we've got to stick together.'

Dory smiled at him. 'Sounds good to me.'

Lucas looked away, reaching blindly for the plate of croissants. Dory's smile was bad for his resolve. And whatever happened next, he needed to do this properly.

He'd been up for hours after Dory went to bed, looking through all the photos responsible for her presence there that holiday, and reading every single gossip column that went with them. Frustratingly, the lighting was so bad in the photos it made the details hard to make out, and with only Tyler facing the camera, identifying the woman from behind was tricky. But Lucas had spent a lot of time over the last day observing Dory, and coupled with Dory's strange admission about her deal with Tyler, he was almost certain that she wasn't the woman in the photo.

Which meant that she – and Tyler – were lying. But why? And who the hell had Tyler actually been with that he thought bringing his assistant home for Christmas was a better idea?

'They ran out!' Felicia stormed into the room, hands waving in disbelief. 'How can a Christmas tree supplier run out of trees?'

'They're out of all trees?' Patrick asked, looking up from his paper for the first time that morning.

'Well, no. They offered us a small seven-footer.' Felicia dropped into her chair. 'As if *that* would fill the space in our hallway.'

Dory's face was an image of carefully studied concern, when Lucas knew she actually had to be thinking, *who calls a seven-foot tree small?*

'So, what are we going to do?' Patrick asked. 'Can we demand some sort of recompense?'

'Perhaps. But that doesn't solve our tree issue.'

'Oh dear,' Dory said, looking surprisingly sympathetic. 'Shall I pour you some coffee?'

Felicia looked surprised, but nodded. 'And quite honestly, I don't have time to deal with this today. There's so much to do before the guests arrive!' she said, sitting down and adding cream to her coffee. 'The caterers will be here any time now to start prepping, and you have to supervise them, you know. No idea about garnishes, some of them. It's quite exhausting. But how can we have the party without a tree?'

'It all sounds very difficult,' Dory said. She wasn't looking at him at all, Lucas realised. He'd expected maybe an eye roll, or secret smile, at his mother's problems, especially after their conversations the night before, but there was nothing. She must suspect he knew the truth. He needed to ask her. He needed to know what was going on.

Because if Dory wasn't actually dating Tyler… well. A whole world of possibilities opened up.

And Lucas knew just how to take advantage of them. 'I'll go and fetch you a tree. Eight or nine foot, right?'

Felicia blinked at him. 'Well, I don't know where you're going to find one on Christmas Eve. We use the best supplier, you know, so if they're out—'

'We live next to a forest, Mother,' Lucas pointed out. 'There's a Christmas Tree Farm up in the hills. I'll drive up and see what they have. They can probably chop me one down then and there.' He grinned. 'And I'll take my axe, just in case.'

'Lucas Alexander you will do no such thing!' Felicia said. 'The last thing this party needs is you showing up missing a few fingers.'

Just as he'd expected. 'I'll tell you what, then. I'll take Dory with me. She can make sure I don't get too axe-happy.'

'Dory?' Felicia said, just as Dory said, 'Me?'

Felicia's gaze swung over to Dory. 'Of course, I'd love to help,' Dory said, just as Lucas had known she would. After all, she was still trying to get into their good books, for some reason. Possibly a pay rise, for all he knew.

'Well… if you're sure,' Felicia said, frowning slightly.

'*You* don't seem very sure,' Lucas pointed out.

'She's probably remembering the last time you chose the tree. We ended up with that miserable thing that shed needles by the bucketload.' Patrick folded his newspaper. 'However, under the circumstances, I recommend that you let them get on with it, Felicia. Tyler too, if he ever surfaces. They can even decorate it, which should keep them out of your way for the day.'

'You know we're not actually children, right?' Lucas asked even though, right then, he almost felt like one. How many years had it been since he last chose and decorated the Alexander family tree on Christmas Eve?

'At Christmas time, we're all children,' Tyler announced, walking in and dropping a kiss on the top of Dory's head. She jumped at the contact, which gave Lucas a strange moment of satisfaction.

'So you'll be coming to fetch the tree too?' Lucas asked, praying Tyler would say no. How was he supposed to get the truth out of Dory if her supposed boyfriend was there?

'Tree? God no.' Tyler grabbed a croissant. 'I've got work to do.'

'On Christmas Eve?' Dory asked. 'But you said…'

'Sorry, honey.' Tyler didn't sound very apologetic, Lucas thought. And had Dory actually flinched at the endearment? God, how had he not figured out what a sham their relationship was before this? 'Something came up.'

'Is that what your phone was ringing about this morning?' Dory asked. '*Someone* seemed very eager to get hold of you.'

Something in the way she said it, the slight edge in her voice that he hadn't heard before, told Lucas there was something more than work going on here. And he was more determined than ever to find out exactly what.

Gulping down the last mouthful of his coffee, Lucas got to his feet. 'Come on, then. If it's just the two of us, we'd better get to work.'

Dory gave him a tight smile and pushed her empty plate away. Had she even managed any breakfast? 'We better had,' she said. 'Not long to go now, after all.'

***

There was no reason for her to be nervous about being alone with Lucas; intellectually, Dory knew that. They'd spent a large portion of the previous evening just the two of them and some cake. This wasn't new, it wasn't weird. He was Tyler's brother, and Lucas still believed that she was his prospective future sister-in-law.

At least, she hoped he did.

That was why she was nervous, she decided, as she climbed into the passenger seat of Lucas's four-by-four: her own paranoia about what she might have said the night before and what Lucas might have inferred. Why was it so impossible to remember the exact wording she'd used, after the event? Had she told Lucas about the deal before or after he asked about the photos?

Of course, that wasn't the only reason. There was also this morning's discovery. It was one thing to lie to Lucas about her relationship with Tyler when all that was at stake was her job and her trip home. Quite another thing now she knew that Tyler was sleeping with Lucas's ex-wife.

What if Lucas went and looked again at the photos? Would he recognise Cheryl? They'd been married, for heaven's sake. He must have more than a passing familiarity with her shape and form. But would it be enough to identify her as the shadowed and hidden woman in the photos? Or would it simply never cross Lucas's mind that his brother would betray him that way?

She hoped not. She hoped that Lucas never had to find out, never had to be hurt like that. Yes, perhaps there was an argument for telling him the truth, but why, when it could only cause him pain? Surely it was much better to get Tyler to stop the craziness and for them all to move on. If Tyler wasn't dating Cheryl then he wouldn't need Dory as a pretend girlfriend, and everything could go back to normal.

Now she just had to convince Tyler of the plan.

'You're applying far too much thought to the purchase of a Christmas tree,' Lucas said, as they turned off the drive to Midfield House and on to the main road. 'Unless there's something else on your mind you want to discuss.'

'No,' Dory said, too quickly. 'Just… you know. The tree.'

'Right.' Somehow, she got the impression that Lucas didn't

believe her.

'So, how far away is this Christmas tree farm?' she asked. Outside the car window, grey and muted-green scenery passed by, edged with a sparkling frost.

'Not far,' Lucas said. 'But the road's a bit windy. There's ginger chews in the glovebox if you need them.' She glanced over at him and he shrugged. 'Freya had some in the pantry. I grabbed them while you were getting your scarf and gloves. They're supposed to be good for motion sickness.'

'Thanks,' Dory said, feeling somehow guiltier than ever.

The car left the main road for a narrower one, a thoroughfare to nowhere that grew thinner and windier as they rose up into the hills. After ten minutes of climbing, Dory reached for the ginger chews, surprised to realise that they really did help.

'I'll have to get some of these for the plane home,' she mumbled.

'Take those,' Lucas said. 'I won't need them.'

Dory nodded, but left them in the glovebox, for the journey home.

Eventually, about ten minutes after Dory felt her ears pop, Lucas turned off the track into a muddy space that appeared to be used as a car park. There were only a couple of other cars there – Dory assumed that most people had put up their trees before the last moment. But a bored-looking Santa stood by a wooden shed with a price board, and there was a small stack of trees wrapped in green netting beside him.

Jumping down from the car, Dory followed Lucas over to the shed, her boots slipping on the mud where the ice had melted. As she slid into place beside him, Lucas grabbed her arm, keeping her upright, and too, too close. The heat of his body warmed her through their clothes, and Dory stepped away quickly. The last thing she needed right now was the confused feelings Lucas's closeness prompted.

Lucas, meanwhile, seemed utterly oblivious to the fact he'd touched her at all. Damn him.

'Eight foot?' Santa asked, shaking his head at Lucas's question. 'They've all gone, last week. Might be some left out in the forest, I guess.' He turned and hollered behind him. 'Evie?'

Dory hid a grin as a grumpy teenager in an elf outfit trotted out from behind the shed. The girl's expression brightened when she spotted Lucas.

'Whadda ya need, Santa?' Evie asked, looking up at Lucas through her lashes.

'These folks need an eight-footer. Want to take them out into the woods, see if you can find one?'

'Sure thing,' Evie said, spinning towards the trees so fast that the bell on her hat jingled. 'Just follow me.'

'See?' Lucas whispered as they walked into the trees. 'Isn't this more fun than watching my mother yell at the caterers?'

'Much,' Dory said. But he was standing too close, and there was something in his voice… What was she missing here?

'Besides, this way we can carry on getting to know each other,' he added, as his longer stride brought him even with her.

Dory swallowed. That, right there, was exactly what she was afraid of.

***

She was nervous; he could tell. Lucas allowed himself a small, satisfied smile. Dory wouldn't let herself look at him, so she'd never notice.

Any uncertainty he'd had about the conclusions he'd reached had vanished. All that was left now was to find out how far Dory was willing to push the charade. How long she'd cling to the story and keep lying to him.

'So, is this you guys' first Christmas together?' Evie asked, from up ahead. Her blonde ponytail swung from side to side as she walked, but not as markedly as her hips. Obviously she hadn't got the hint yet that he had other things on his mind than a pretty, probably underage, girl. And what he was about to do doubtless wouldn't help. On the other hand, maybe Dory would get jealous…

'Oh, we're not together,' he said. 'Dory here is practically my sister-in-law. She's dating my brother, and he just brought her home to spend Christmas with the family.' He added enough emphasis to the last few words that Evie could hardly miss his meaning.

The elf spun around, walking backwards through the mud, eyes wide. 'Wow. Do you think he's going to propose?'

Dory stumbled over a tree root, and Lucas grabbed her arm once again to steady her. This would be hilarious if she wasn't lying to him and his family about everything. Lucas couldn't shake the thought that if Tyler wasn't really dating his assistant… then the truth must be even worse. He needed to find out what it was. As soon as he got Dory to admit the lies.

'Um, I don't think so,' Dory said. 'Not yet, anyway. We've only been together a few months…' Evie looked far more disappointed by this than Dory.

Lucas spotted a chance to push his advantage and went for it. 'Actually, you never told me how you and Tyler got together.'

'I bet it's really romantic,' Evie added. 'Tell us!' Lucas had no idea if all elves had such romantic tendencies, but he was grateful for Evie's. She was making his mission a whole lot easier.

'Well… Tyler's my boss, actually,' Dory started, and Evie gasped.

'So you had to keep it a secret!' Evie bounced a little on the toes of her elf boots. They'd stopped walking altogether now, not that Lucas minded.

'Yeah. But, um, we were working together every day, taking business trips, late-night flights, that sort of thing. And we just grew… closer.'

Close enough for Tyler to persuade her to be his fake girlfriend for the holiday, anyway.

'And then?' he asked. 'How did you get from that to photos of you in a national magazine with Tyler's hand up your skirt?'

Colour flooded Dory's cheeks as she stepped back from him. Evie's excited expression had faded into a frown, and Lucas suspected he'd lost her support entirely.

'I don't think that's any of your damn business.' Striding forward, Dory waited for Evie to catch her up then added, 'Now, where are these eight-foot trees? I'd like to get back to my boyfriend at some point this Christmas Eve.'

Dammit. He'd pushed too far and she'd clammed up. He'd hoped the direct approach might fluster the truth out of her. Instead it had effectively ended his fact-finding mission.

He trudged after Dory and Evie, crunching through the frozen mud and leaves, until they found a small selection of taller trees, chopped down but not net-wrapped yet. Dory stood back as he chose the one most likely not to offend his mother, then slung it on to a sledge to drag it back through the woods to Santa and the car.

Dory didn't speak to him once. But, Lucas decided, that was okay.

It just meant it was time for Plan B.

Chapter 7

'Now, these decorations have been handed down through generations of Alexander women,' Felicia said, holding one of the boxes close to her chest. 'They're very valuable. And fragile.'

'Lucas and I will be very careful with them,' Dory promised. She wasn't entirely sure how she'd agreed to decorate, as well as fetch, the tree. After the stony silence of the drive back to Midfield House, tree bouncing on the roof, she'd been hoping to hide out in her room until it was time to get ready for the party. But Felicia had been waiting in the hallway with boxes of antique decorations, and before she'd been able to make her excuses, Lucas had volunteered her. Again.

She was getting a little bit sick of that, actually.

Dory reached out to take the box of decorations, and Felicia leant back. Dory let her hand fall, and glanced back at Lucas who, having set the ridiculously oversized tree into its stand in the hallway, was now stringing lights around it, without waiting for the branches to drop and settle. He wasn't even looking at her, and still Dory got the impression that he was up to something. Just biding his time before he attacked again.

'They were bought for Patrick's great-great-aunt by an English lord,' Felicia went on. Did she expect Dory to be impressed by her own country's aristocracy? Clearly she hadn't spent enough time reading the British gossip magazines.

'I'm sure they're beautiful,' Dory said. 'Do you think maybe I could see them?' The boxes looked awfully small, even if there were six of them. Could there possibly be enough decorations in there to cover the ginormous thing Lucas had dragged in from the forest?

'Of course.' Felicia gave her a bright, brittle smile. 'Let's set them out on the table over here.'

Placing the box on the console table next to the tree with great care, Felicia lifted the lid, and Dory gave a reverential sigh. However crazy protective Felicia was over the things, Dory couldn't deny that they *were* beautiful.

'They're incredible,' Dory said, earning a real smile from Felicia for once. 'They'll look stunning on the tree.'

'And you'll be careful?' Felicia asked. 'Only, they're a tradition in the family…'

'We'll be careful, Mother,' Lucas said, putting his arm around Felicia and leading her towards the kitchen door. 'So trust us and leave us to it. I'm sure Freya needs your supervision on something.'

The thought of what the maid might be screwing up elsewhere was apparently enough to make Felicia forget about leaving precious heirlooms in the charge of the interloper, and Lucas shut the door behind her before she could change her mind.

Leaving Dory alone with Lucas again. Just what she didn't want. Dory didn't know what he was playing at, but the way he looked at her, as if he could see through every lie she'd ever told, made her intensely nervous.

Where the hell was Tyler? Why couldn't he help with this? Maybe then Lucas would stop making her feel so on edge.

Of course, it didn't help that she really, really wanted to find out what would happen if she just told Lucas the truth.

Looking for a distraction, Dory reached into the box and lifted out the first decoration. A handblown glass teardrop, streaked with blues and silvers. 'They're so delicate.'

'Don't you start,' Lucas said. 'We'll never get this damn thing decorated if you start acting like mother about them.'

'Hey, you're the one who volunteered us for this gig,' she said, putting down the first decoration and picking up another. She wasn't going to look at him. Wasn't going to give him the satisfaction of knowing he got under her skin.

'Yeah, but I had an ulterior motive.' Dory froze. Dammit. Against her better judgement, she looked up. His smile and raised eyebrow didn't quite match his tone. She swallowed. What was he playing at? What did he think he knew? What had he guessed?

'And what's that, then?' she asked, heart drumming in her chest.

'I wanted to get you alone.' He'd moved closer, suddenly, close enough that her blood hummed.

'You've had me alone all morning,' she pointed out, turning away again.

'No,' Lucas said, patiently. 'I've had you and Santa and the elf and the tree. Not what I need.'

'Didn't seem to stop you asking all manner of inappropriate questions.'

'It stopped you answering them, though.' His voice was soft, like he was talking to a frightened kitten. Gentling her along. 'Dory—'

She spun round, cutting him off. 'What? What do you want to know? Or do you just want to tease me and make me feel even more uncomfortable here than I do anyway? If you've got a real question, ask it.'

He watched her for a long moment, then nodded. 'Okay, then. Why are you pretending to be in a relationship with my brother?'

***

'What do you know?' Dory asked, her face pale in the bright white lights from the tree. 'I mean, what are you talking about?'

'Too late, sweetheart,' Lucas said. 'You already slipped. I know you're not the woman in those photographs, for a start. Want to tell me who she is?'

Dory shook her head, staring down at the decoration in her hands. 'He never told me.'

'But he convinced you to come along and take part in this little play-acting thing he's got going on?' She nodded. 'What did he promise you?'

'A trip home.' She looked up, eyes bright and words coming too fast. 'I couldn't afford to go home for Christmas, you see, and he knew I really wanted to go. So he said if I'd do this, come here for a few days, he'd give me two weeks off and a plane ticket home for the 27th. I couldn't… I just wanted to go home.'

Her expression, pleading with him to understand, made something inside his chest ache. Had he ever wanted to go home that badly? Even when he was in boarding school? He didn't think so. 'That doesn't explain why he didn't just bring his *actual* girlfriend.'

Dory's gaze darted away again. 'He just said that bringing her would be worse even than your parents finding out he was dating his assistant.'

God, that really didn't sound good. 'And you didn't demand to know who she was?' He would have. Would never have gotten mixed up in something like this without knowing the full score.

'I just wanted to go home,' Dory said again.

Lucas sucked in a breath, then let it out slowly. 'Okay. Okay, I understand.' He gave her a lopsided smile. 'And actually, it's kind of a relief.'

'It is?'

'Yeah.'

'Why?'

Could he say it? Should he? Lucas stared at her, waiting to hear what he had to say, her wide eyes curious now, rather than afraid. Screw it. He'd come this far. 'Because it's kinda bad form to fall for your brother's girlfriend.'

Her breath came out in a whoosh. 'You're… I mean, you… You too?'

You too? With those two little words, he knew he wasn't alone in this. That he hadn't imagined the connection between them, in the car, or eating cake late last night. Even fetching the damn tree that morning. She felt it too.

Relief flooded through him and, without thinking, he stepped forward, needing to be closer, but she dodged back. 'What is it?' he asked.

Slim fingers held up the ribbon of one of his mother's precious decorations. 'Let me put this out of harm's way.'

He chuckled, watching her place it carefully on the tree. Then she turned back to him, lower lip caught between her teeth. 'Lucas… we still can't…' she stopped and tucked her hair behind her ears. 'I'm here as Tyler's girlfriend.'

'Pretend girlfriend,' he clarified.

'It still has its responsibilities,' she said, with a small smile. 'We're in the main hallway of your parents' house, Lucas. If someone walked in here…'

'Yeah. Yeah, okay.' She was right. Of course she was right. Whatever secret Tyler was keeping… he needed to find that out before he could blow apart this fake relationship they'd set up. He needed to know what trouble Lucas was in, and how he could fix it, without getting dragged back into the family responsibilities.

One step at a time. Talk to Tyler. Fix the problem. Go home to his farm and check on the restaurant. Take a trip to the city to see Dory, as soon as she got back from Britain. And then…

There was only one problem with the plan, Lucas thought, as his body swayed closer to Dory's again, almost without his permission. He never had been a patient man.

***

She should step back. She really should step back. Move away, out of the aura of possibility that Lucas projected. She couldn't be here, couldn't do this. Her job, her trip home, keeping up the illusion of her perfect life, everything depended on her being Tyler's perfect girlfriend this weekend. She needed to stop this.

But Dory didn't step back.

Lucas's hand wrapped around her hip, pulling her closer, his lips descending on hers, firm and decisive, as if telling her it wasn't worth arguing with him.

Not that she particularly wanted to.

Her hands moved up to his chest, feeling the strength of him through his sweater, snaking around to his back as the small gap between them disappeared completely. Suddenly she didn't care how much she shouldn't be doing this.

Lucas's grip tightened as both arms wrapped around her waist, holding her close, and he deepened the kiss. Dory's whole body tightened, desperate for more. If it weren't for all these pesky clothes – and her boss and his family in the house...

Reality snapped back into place, and reluctantly Dory pulled away from Lucas's lips. Breathing harder than seemed reasonable from just one kiss, she looked up into his eyes as he rested his forehead against hers, arms still tight around her.

'We can't,' she said, voice soft.

'Yet.' Her heart lifted a little at the word, and the husky way he said it.

'Yet,' she agreed. 'I'll be back in the country in a couple of weeks. Tyler will have to break it off then – or I will. The deal was only for these few days. Once I'm back...' What? What would happen next? What did she even want to happen – besides getting Lucas very naked in her bed?

'I'll call you,' Lucas said, only that didn't sound like enough. To him either, it seemed, as he went on, 'I'll visit. Or you can come out to the farm. See the restaurant.'

'See where this goes,' Dory interpreted.

'Yeah. Exactly.'

She smiled. 'I'd like that.'

She was still close enough to feel his chest sink as he let out a breath of relief. 'Good. That's... good.'

It took a huge effort, but Dory made herself step back, and Lucas's arms fell away in acceptance. He gave her a lopsided smile and scrubbed a hand over his short-cropped hair.

'So, for now I guess we just… decorate the tree.' Dory looked back at the oversized fir, naked but for a few strings of fairy lights and one small, glass teardrop. How long had they been doing this, anyway? What if someone came to check on them?

'Yeah,' Lucas agreed. 'And I find out exactly who that woman in the photo with Tyler really was.' He shook his head. 'Whatever he's gotten himself into this time, I need to fix it before it becomes a thing, and Dad decides he can't be trusted and I get dragged back into the family business again.'

A chill settled over Dory's spine, and she wrapped her arms around her middle to try and find some of the warmth she'd felt in Lucas's arms. She didn't know exactly how Lucas felt about his ex-wife, but from Tyler's determination to keep the relationship a secret, she guessed his reaction probably wouldn't be good.

'Do you have any idea who it could be?' she asked.

Lucas raised his eyes to heaven. 'With Tyler, it could be anyone. Maybe the daughter of a competitor? Or some scandal-prone minor celebrity? Tyler's never been exactly… discerning in his relationships. But if he figured that risking Dad finding out that he was dating his assistant was a better option… well, it can't be good.'

Except it wasn't a business scandal Tyler was afraid of, Dory knew now. It was a family one. And if Lucas was determined to find out the truth…

'Let's get this tree finished first,' she said, trying to sound light-hearted when, in truth, her heart felt as heavy as Christmas pudding.

She needed to talk to Tyler. Needed to get him to confess to his brother, to figure a way out of this mess for all of them.

Before Lucas found out on his own.

***

By the time the tree was finished, Dory wasn't sure she could take the frustration of being in the same room with Lucas much longer. Part of her was desperate to just yell 'Tyler's sleeping with your ex-wife!' and damn the consequences. Another, equally loud and insistent part, just wanted to kiss him again, maybe even more, and with a similar regard for what happened next.

Stepping back, Dory took in their handiwork. The tiny glass antique decorations sparkled and shone, reflecting the fairy lights and sending twinkles of lights cascading over the walls.

'It does look beautiful,' Dory said.

Lucas placed the lid on the last of the now-empty wooden boxes that had held the decorations. 'It looks like a picture from a magazine. Just like the rest of this house.'

Dory turned, frowning at the tinge of bitterness in his voice. 'You don't like picture-perfect?'

'I don't like fake,' Lucas said. 'And I don't like the idea of living a life just to fit someone else's idea of perfect.'

Dory glanced away, thinking of her own, fake-perfect life. 'It's just a tree, Lucas.'

'Yeah.' He huffed a small laugh. 'Yeah, it is. Sorry. Just… thinking about Tyler again.'

'Think about it tomorrow,' Dory suggested. 'We've got tonight's party to get through first.'

Lucas groaned. 'It truly *is* the most wonderful time of the year.'

'Well, I have to admit, I'm a little excited.'

'Don't be.'

'I am!' Dory insisted. 'A famous Alexander Christmas Eve party, and I get to attend. It'll be a story to tell the grandkids.' Lucas's gaze shot up to meet hers and Dory's eyes widened. 'Not that I'm saying… I mean, not… I wasn't thinking…'

'You weren't thinking they would be my grandkids, too,' Lucas said, putting her out of her misery.

'They were hypothetical grandkids.'

'Well, yeah. We haven't even slept together. Yet.'

Something buzzed through her blood at the word 'yet.' 'No. We haven't.' Why couldn't she look away from his eyes?

After a long moment, Lucas grinned and dropped his stare. 'Besides, if they were mine, attending a family party would hardly be such a big deal.'

Dory forced a laugh. 'There is that.' A thought popped into her mind, growing and growing. If she and Lucas pursued an actual relationship… she might have to visit Midfield House – and the Alexander clan – again. Which made it all the more important that Tyler sorted out this whole affair amicably.

Right now.

'Well, if we're done here, I need to go call home before I start getting ready for the party,' Dory said.

'Yeah, I should probably do the same,' Lucas said. 'Check that the farm and restaurant are coping without me.'

'I'm sure they're simply withering.' Lucas returned her grin and, before she even registered what was happening, he had one arm wrapped around her waist again, hauling her close. 'We said—'

'Shush,' Lucas murmured. 'Just one more kiss.'

He leant in, and Dory's whole body strained to get closer. Just one more kiss. How could she possibly say no to that?

***

It was a good fifteen minutes before Lucas finally let Dory slip away up the stairs, away from his arms and his kisses. He stood in the hallway, watching her skip lightly up the steps, wondering exactly how much his brother would hate him if he just dragged his assistant/fake girlfriend off to spend Christmas on his farm, instead of here, pretending not to care as his mother passive-aggressively insulted her again.

He sighed. No. He needed to talk to Tyler first.

'Have you finished?' Felicia click-clacked into the hallway in her heels, a slight frown line marring her forehead. She stopped a few feet away. 'Oh. It looks…' Lucas waited for the inevitable complaint, but it never came. 'Perfect. Thank you.'

He blinked at his mother, trying to process what had just happened. 'Uh, well, Dory did most of it.'

A slight twist at the corner of her mouth at the sound of Dory's name told him that a perfectly decorated tree was unlikely to change Felicia's opinion of Tyler's supposed girlfriend. He wondered if that would change were he the one to bring her home for the holidays next year.

'Well, I'm sure I'm very grateful to you both.' Felicia glanced down at her watch. 'Now, time is getting on. I'm going to need you to start collecting guests from the station before long.'

For once, Lucas wished his mother would actually use her immense wealth and staff, then felt bad for being selfish. 'Don't we have a driver who does that sort of thing?'

'Of course we do.' Felicia gave him an impatient look. 'And he'll be running trips, too. But for our oldest friends… you know they like to see you.'

They didn't, particularly, Lucas knew. But Felicia liked for them to see him. To show that he was still here, still part of the family, not wasting away drunk every night after his divorce, as some gossip rags would have it.

'Fine,' he said. 'Give me a list of train times?'

'It's already in your room.' Felicia headed towards the dining room then stopped in the doorway, turning back towards him. 'Oh, before you go and get changed – could you hang the mistletoe for tonight?' She waved a hand at the table behind him and he saw the stems with their glossy green leaves and bright-white berries, waiting to trap unsuspecting party guests into locking lips.

He hadn't even needed it for Dory, though. The need to kiss her had been overwhelming. And he was pretty sure he wasn't imagining that it had felt the same for her, too.

Maybe, just maybe, if he got a quiet moment, he could catch her again later…

'I'll put it up,' he promised. 'Then I'll take a shower, put on the monkey suit, and go start fetching guests.' Talking to Tyler would have to wait a few hours. But no longer.

'Thank you,' Felicia said, her smile warmer than it had been since he arrived. She always liked him best when he was doing what he was told.

Standing on the lower steps of the stairs, Lucas reached up and pinned the mistletoe into its usual place, in the centre of the hall. But he kept back one stem, carrying it upstairs to his room with him. Just in case.

Chapter 8

Tyler wasn't in their room when Dory got back, which, she decided, was probably just as well, since her lips were still tingling from Lucas's kisses. And it gave her time to figure out what she was going to say to her boss, too. It was a delicate situation, after all. *So, you're sleeping with your ex-sister-in-law?* probably wouldn't go down too well.

The only problem was she found it kinda hard to focus on the very serious conversation she needed to have with Tyler, when her mind kept getting invaded with thoughts of his brother. The way Lucas's hands had gripped her hips, hauling her close. The feel of his chest under her hands. His back, his shoulders, his lips…

Focus, Dory. She needed to sort things out with Tyler so she could get back to the good stuff with his brother. Simple as that.

Because if Lucas found out that she'd known Tyler was sleeping with Cheryl before Tyler confessed all… well, that kind of thing tended to put a dampener on the sexy times.

In the end, she decided to call home while she waited for Tyler, and tried not to cry as she heard the sounds of her traditional family Christmas Eve – so unlike the black-tie traditions of the Alexanders – in the background.

'Are you really still working on Christmas Eve?' her sister, Molly, asked when their dad handed her the phone. 'Or have you met

83

some super-hot guy and made plans to spend the whole Christmas period in bed?'

A bit of both, Dory wanted to say, but didn't. 'Yeah, my boss needed me here, so I'm still working.' Technically true, as long as Molly didn't ask where 'here' was.

'Poor thing. We've just polished off the last of dinner. Dad's cracking open more wine for mulling – he's mixing his own special spice blend again this year. And Mum has the mince pies in the oven, so it's all business as usual here.'

Dory's stomach actually rumbled at the very thought of her mother's mince pies. 'Wish I was there.' In the background, Dory heard her brother complaining about having to listen to Cliff Richard again. She wondered how horrified he'd be if he knew she'd voluntarily included it on her Christmas playlist.

'We do too,' Molly said. 'But New Year, right? I think Mum and Dad are planning a bit of a party here, to celebrate having you home. Give you a chance to see everyone.'

'That sounds brilliant.' Just a couple more days and she'd be home. And for once, thinking about coming back to the States again didn't give her the same rolling wave of homesickness she usually got. Because the good old US of A had Lucas Alexander in it...

'Well, I'll let you get back to work,' Molly said. 'You'll call tomorrow, right? And we'll see you in a few days, yeah?'

'I will. Can't wait. Merry Christmas, Mol.' Dory pressed the button to end the call and flopped back on to the bed. Just a few more days. She could make it that long without inappropriately seducing Lucas. Right?

She headed for the shower – slightly chilly, just in case – and pulled out her dress for the party. Long, red-wine coloured, and a little bit slinky. Smart but sexy. Hopefully sophisticated enough to satisfy Felicia and Patrick, expensive-looking enough that people would believe Tyler would date her, and sexy enough that Lucas would spend the entire evening imagining slipping her out of it.

Perfect.

The party guests wouldn't be arriving for a couple of hours, but if she was all ready she could go downstairs and see what she could do to help. She had a feeling that, after her chat with Tyler, she might want to be somewhere away from him for a while, anyway.

Tyler finally returned to the room just as she was putting the finishing touches to her make-up. Shoving her lipstick back into her clutch bag, she swivelled round on the dressing table stool and smiled up at him. 'You're back!'

He blinked at her. 'You're… ready? Already?'

'I thought I'd see if your mum needed a hand with anything downstairs,' Dory said, still smiling manically. 'But I, uh, need to talk to you about something first.'

'Oh God.' Tyler dropped to sprawl on the bed. 'That doesn't sound good. Can I just remind you that I spent all night on that sofa, so I ache like hell, and I'm still hung-over from drinking brandy with my father last night. Are you sure this can't wait?'

'Actually, it really can't,' Dory said, apologetically. 'And it kind of has something to do with you sleeping on the sofa last night.'

Tyler sat bolt upright. 'Look, Dory, I was joking about sharing the bed. I don't think it would be very appropriate. I mean, you're my employee. And I'm involved with someone. Seriously involved.'

'I know,' Dory said. 'She called this morning. Repeatedly.'

Colour faded from Tyler's already-pale cheeks. 'She did?'

'Yeah. And you were passed out cold. So… I answered the phone.'

'Shit.'

'So, I guess I finally understand why pretending to date your assistant was a better option than bringing your actual girlfriend home for Christmas,' Dory joked, but it fell flat.

'Look, you don't understand. Cheryl and I…'

'Are going to have to explain this to Lucas. Quickly.'

'What? No! Not a chance.'

Dory's frustration level rose. 'Why not? If you guys are serious, he'll have to find out eventually.'

'But not now. Not here,' Tyler said, firmly.

'You have to tell him, Tyler. Or I will.'

Tyler stilled, staring at her. 'And why do you suddenly care about what my brother does and doesn't deserve to know?'

Heat hit her face as she blushed. Staring down at her navy-polished nails, Dory said, 'It's the decent thing to do.'

'But that's not why you want me to do it, is it?' Tyler's voice sounded tight, like he was holding something in. 'So, what? You've fallen for him over a snowy walk in the forest and some Christmas ornaments and you want to get out of our deal? You're really going to risk your trip home for one night with my brother? Are you sure? Because I can tell you, Cheryl says he wasn't all that much to write home about.'

Dory didn't believe *that* for a moment, but that wasn't the point. She needed to keep her focus here, and not get distracted by thoughts of Lucas in bed. 'He already knows, Tyler. That we're not really dating, I mean. He could tell it wasn't me in the photos.'

'So what did you tell him?'

'That you'd asked me to come and cover for you this week. That you hadn't told me who the woman in the photos was.'

Tyler raised an eyebrow. 'Very clever. Not quite a lie, but not quite the truth either.' He tutted. 'Keeping secrets already. Doesn't bode well for the two of you, does it?'

Weariness settled over Dory. She just wanted this to be over, already. 'Look, he has a right to know the truth. We don't have to tell your parents, and I'm happy to play the dutiful girlfriend for the next couple of days. But after that, after I get back from my trip home, I want to be free to date anyone I like – including your brother, potentially. So he has to know the truth.'

But Tyler just shook his head. 'Not a chance. I'll tell him when I'm good and ready, and I can promise you now, that won't be this weekend.'

'Then I'll tell him.'

'No, you won't.' He looked so smug, so sure, that Dory's jaw ached from clenching it, biting back the names she wanted to call him. 'Because if you do, I guarantee you he'll forget all about your little flirtation and punch me out in the middle of my parent's party. Which, I think we can both agree, will not constitute you holding up your half of the bargain. Which means you won't get this.' He reached into the bedside-table drawer and pulled out her plane ticket home, bow stuck on the envelope. 'So, just in case, I'll hang on to it, I think. Until we're on our way out of here, the day after tomorrow.'

Dory's heart clenched as she watched him tuck the ticket in his pocket. 'He deserves to know, Tyler.'

'Maybe. But not today. Not if you want your trip home. Or a job when you get back again.'

She wasn't sure she even *wanted* the job, after this. 'Why are you doing this?'

Tyler's shoulders sagged, and he gave her a tired smile. 'Believe it or not, I'm not trying to make you miserable. I'm just trying to save my family from imploding.'

'I think you might have lost your shot at that when you started sleeping with your brother's ex-wife.' Tyler shrugged, as if to say 'what can you do?' Watching him, Dory felt compelled to ask the question that had been in her mind since she answered the phone that morning. 'Are you in love with her?'

God, he looked so tired. 'Of course I am. I always have been.'

'Even when she was married to Lucas?'

'Long before,' Tyler admitted, and Dory couldn't help but feel a little bit sorry for him. 'And I'm sorry, Dory. But I can't let you ruin this for me.'

***

Lucas tweaked his bow tie in one last attempt to get the damn thing to lie straight. He looked like a waiter, but he supposed chauffeur wasn't all that far off. It fitted how he felt at these events, anyway. Out of place, and only there to perform a service – to prove to all and sundry that the Alexander family were still as close a unit as ever.

Even if it was a complete lie.

The rap on his door surprised him and he knocked the tie wonky again. Swearing under his breath he tugged on the bow and pulled it out, leaving the tie dangling around his collar. He'd fix it later.

Yanking the door open, he expected to see his mother, come to check he was leaving for the station.

His breath caught in his chest. Not his mother. Not anything like.

'You look incredible.' Lucas let his gaze trail down from the pink of her cheeks, over the line of her collarbones, the curves of her breasts, waist and hips, all the way down the silky fall of her dress to the high heels on her feet. God, he wanted to see her legs. Wanted to see every last inch of her.

'You're looking pretty… great yourself.' At Dory's breathy words, he pulled his attention back up to her lips, red and plump and made for kissing.

'Is everything okay?' he asked, trying to keep his mind on her conversation, rather than what he wanted to do to her body.

'I needed to…' She bit her lip, and an irrational hope rose up in Lucas as to exactly what Dory might need. 'Can I come in?'

Lucas stepped aside, and she slipped past, into his room. Just where he wanted her…

The mistletoe lay half-forgotten on the table under the window and, as he shut the door behind him, Lucas saw Dory pick it up, twisting the stems between her fingers. 'Had plans for this, did you?'

With a shrug, Lucas moved towards her, his bigger hands covering hers completely. 'Hopes. Not plans.'

She looked up at him. 'So what were you hoping?'

'That I'd get to do this again.' Sliding one arm around her waist, Lucas pulled Dory to him, bending his head to meet her lips with his. She tasted every bit as sweet as she had earlier, and the dress let him feel every curve of her body, close against his. He wondered if she could feel how hard he was for her, through the fabric of his suit. Wondered, if he angled his leg so, if he could feel the heat of her...

'Oh God,' Dory moaned against his mouth as he slid his knee between her thighs, using his free hand to hitch up her skirt. 'This wasn't... I didn't...'

'Want me to stop?' Lucas murmured, in between placing kisses along her throat.

'God no!' Her arms wrapped around him, emphasising her words, and he had to kiss her again, deep and desperate. When she finally broke away, he was breathless, mindless, aware of only one thing.

'I really, really want to make love to you,' he whispered, mouth against her ear.

He didn't pull back, didn't want to see any indecision or doubt on her face. He knew the reasons for that, and they weren't to do with him, or with her not wanting to be here. But right now, he couldn't care less about Tyler's problems and schemes. All he cared about was Dory, and the desperate need to get her into his bed.

'Please,' she said, softly. 'God, yes, please.'

That was all he needed.

***

Lucas's kisses were intoxicating. Dory couldn't help but lose herself in them, the dizzy way they moved from her lips to her neck to the curve of her breasts above the neckline of her dress. Had she ever felt this desperate, this out of control, with Ewen? If she had, she couldn't remember it. This feeling of fate, the inevitability of this moment, was entirely new to her. As if the bizarre set of circumstances that had brought her here simply couldn't have happened any other way.

Giving in to destiny, Dory ran her hands over the broadness

of Lucas's back, feeling every muscle through his shirt, thankful he hadn't put his jacket on yet. Even the thin cotton was too much separation for her. She wanted nothing between them, no barriers at all.

Except secrets.

Dory shook the thought away, focusing on the feel of him under her hands instead, letting her hands roam lower, holding him close against her body. Lucas let out a low groan, in between kisses, and she couldn't help but feel powerful, as if he were as lost in this moment as she was – and equally unable to control it.

Tugging her towards the bed, Lucas reached around and unzipped her dress, so by the time they reached the edge of the mattress the silky fabric was already pooled around her feet, leaving her in only her best lingerie, stockings and heels.

Lucas took in the view, and Dory's cheeks grew warm watching the heat in his eyes. God, she wanted this. Her whole body ached for him. And yeah, she knew they needed to talk, that she had things she had to tell him… But that would ruin this perfect moment and, quite simply, she couldn't stand to lose this. Not when she was so close to having him…

'God, you're beautiful.' Lucas brought one hand up to run across her shoulder, down her arm, to her waist. Gently, he pushed her down to sit on the edge of the bed, kneeling between her legs, one finger hooked in the edge of her knickers.

Dory swallowed. Hard.

Telling Lucas about Cheryl could definitely wait until later.

Later turned out to be quite some time away.

Warm and dozy in Lucas's arms, Dory squinted across his broad chest at the clock on the bedside table.

'Don't look at it.' Lucas's voice was low and husky. 'If we don't know what time it is, we can't be late.'

'I'm not sure it works that way,' Dory said, but let her head drop back down to rest against his shoulder anyway. 'Your mother is going to kill me.'

'I'll protect you,' he said, tightening his grip on her naked body. 'Besides, she'll kill me first. I'm supposed to be picking up guests from the station right now.'

Dory winced, and tried to rise, but Lucas kept her plastered against his side. 'We should get up,' she mumbled against his skin. 'I need another shower now. And to redo my make-up.'

'Don't wanna.' Pressing kisses against the top of her head, Lucas's hand roamed down over her hip, cupping her bottom as he held her close.

'Neither do I,' Dory whispered back. Her body still thrummed with slow satisfaction, but her mind was returning rapidly to reality. Fate, destiny, inevitability – they were all excuses. Just another lie to tell herself to get what she wanted. She still had to tell Lucas the truth, but Tyler was right about one thing – she couldn't do it now. Quite apart from ruining the Alexander Christmas Eve party, she couldn't let the memory of this moment be ruined by what would follow.

After Christmas, she'd tell him. Before she left for Liverpool. Then he would have time to sort out his feelings – and his brother – before she got back, and his parents would be none the wiser. Perfect.

Somewhere downstairs, there were voices. Clinking glasses. The party had started. Their precious, stolen moment was over, for now.

Reluctantly, Dory pulled away, sitting up slowly to let her body catch up with the new plan. Most of her still seemed to be luxuriating in the memory of what they'd just done. Lucas's hand fell away, and she stood up, smiling back down at him. She could still feel his hands, his mouth, his body, over every inch of hers. God, they had to do that again. Really soon.

'Mind if I borrow your shower?' she asked. Tyler might still be in their room, and she really didn't fancy facing him again alone just yet. She had enough make-up in her evening bag to repair her face, she hoped.

Lucas waved a hand towards the bathroom lazily. 'Go ahead.' He grinned at her. 'But I'd lock the door, if you don't want me joining you.'

Fifteen minutes later, thanked to the locked door, Dory was ready to face the party. Lucas, however, was still in bed.

'You go down first,' he said, sitting up at last. The blankets fell away from his chest and Dory bit her lip just looking at the glory of him naked. 'I'll follow in a bit.'

Dory nodded. 'Good idea.'

'You realise you're still here, right?' Lucas asked, eyebrow raised.

'I'm going. Any moment.' She allowed herself one last, long look, then shook her head and tore her gaze away. 'I'm gone.' Striding across the room as fast as she could in the ridiculous heels – the only ones she owned that went with the dress – Dory stepped out on to the landing, pulling the door to behind her. She sucked a deep breath in, listening to the sounds of the party below, louder now. It was time to face the music.

***

'Where the hell have you been?' Tyler whispered, the moment she made it downstairs. His hand went automatically to her waist, holding her close like a good fake boyfriend should. Dory plastered on a smile for the guests milling around the giant Christmas tree in the hallway, but all she could think was how very different it felt to be standing so close to Tyler, rather than his brother.

'Sorry,' she said, even though she wasn't. 'I got caught up calling home. They're all drinking mulled wine and everyone wanted to wish me a happy Christmas Eve.'

'Whatever,' Tyler said. Still angry from earlier, then. 'Come on, Mum's been telling everyone about you, so now there's a whole list of people waiting to meet you. It's show time, honey.'

'Then let's go,' Dory said. She could face anyone right now, still on a high after sex with Lucas. And maybe later, once everyone had gone, she and Lucas could find a quiet corner and some mulled wine of their own…

Twenty minutes later, her enthusiasm was starting to fade. She'd smiled, she'd feigned interest, she'd nodded politely… and every time she'd felt the eyes of the guest she was talking to slide away, either back to Tyler or over her shoulder, looking for somebody else. Tyler hadn't seemed to notice, probably because they were all still engaged in conversation with him. His hand had stayed at her waist the whole evening, an unwelcome reminder of their charade.

And worst of all, there was still no sign of Lucas. How long did the man take to shower, anyway?

'Oh, look, you two!' One of Felicia's friends – Dory had lost all track of names by now – pointed up above them. 'Mistletoe!'

Dory stared up. So that was where Lucas had got it. He must have been hanging it for his mother. And now she was trapped under it with his brother. Perfect.

'So there is.' Tyler sounded about as enthusiastic as she felt, but he turned towards her anyway, looping his hands around her waist. 'Pucker up, honey.'

Oh, the romance.

Tyler lowered his lips to meet hers, chaste and dry, and behind her, Dory heard the front door open.

'So sorry we're late,' a woman's voice said, too loudly. 'Only I'm afraid, Felicia, your driver never made it to the station. Might be the weather – it's just started snowing out there, you know. I said we should call, but Cheryl insisted that we get a taxi, and you know what these cab drivers are like. We've been all around the houses to get here!'

They both froze as the woman said 'Cheryl', and Tyler started to pull back. Which meant Dory could see the staircase over his shoulder again.

Could see Lucas standing there, staring at them.

Dory's eyes widened as Lucas looked away, and his expression turned hard and stony. She wanted to run to him, but Tyler's arms were still around her bloody waist and she was still supposed to be his girlfriend and – oh God! – was Cheryl there?

'Tyler? What the hell?' Well, that answered that question. Cheryl's voice was almost as loud as her mother's.

Too late, Tyler's arms fell away and he darted past her. 'Angel, I can explain! What are you even doing here?'

'I was invited.' The pretty brunette folded her arms over her chest. 'I thought it would be a good time to announce our engagement.'

'Your… God. The woman in those photos.' Lucas's voice rang out across the silence of the crowd as he made his way down the stairs. 'I knew it wasn't Dory, but I never thought… my ex-wife, Tyler?'

'Emphasis on the "ex",' Cheryl said, but Lucas ignored her. Ignored the crowd of people watching their every move, taking in every moment of the drama.

Instead, he just stared at Dory. 'And you knew.'

Chapter 9

Dory's throat tightened, her eyes burning. How had this happened? She'd been so sure she'd found a way out, a way to keep everything perfect. Unable to bring herself to speak, Dory nodded miserably.

Anger settled on to Lucas's face like a mask, hard and unyielding. 'I trusted you. Hell, I slept with you! I thought we were starting something. And you were lying to me the whole time.' He kept his voice low, but Dory knew there was no way anyone had missed what he said.

'Not the whole time!' Dory forced the words out. She had to make him understand. 'Lucas, you have to let me explain.'

'I don't… Has anything you told me been the truth? God, I don't even know who you are.'

'That's what I've been asking,' Cheryl put in, but no one seemed to be listening.

'Just let me tell you my side,' Dory pleaded, but Lucas shook his head.

'I don't want to hear it. Not now. I need to fix this. Figure it out.' He turned to Tyler and Cheryl and seemed to notice, for the first time, the true extent of their audience. Every single one of the Alexanders' party guests had crowded into the hallway to witness the spectacle. Glaring at his brother, he said, 'Let's take this into the library.'

Tyler nodded and, holding Cheryl's hand, led her towards the library, murmuring reassurances as he went. But when Dory made to follow, Lucas stopped her with a look. 'Not you,' he said, voice cold. 'This is between me and my brother.'

And then he was gone, the library door shut behind him, leaving Dory alone with the crowd of fascinated socialites, and Felicia and Patrick Alexander.

After a moment of stunned silence, Felicia clapped her hands. 'I think nibbles are being served in the dining room, everyone!' A few people moved, but many stayed, eyes still on Dory. Could they see the way her heart thumped? As if it were making the most of its last few beats before it broke. Any moment now, her whole body might just fall apart, and all she could do was stare at the library door, hoping against hope that Lucas might suddenly appear through it and rescue her.

But he didn't.

Felicia sidled close, while still smiling and ushering people towards the dining room. 'I don't know who you really are, or what your intentions were in being here, but I suggest that you go and pack your bags.' Her voice was a whisper, but there was no mistaking the edge in it. 'I'll have a taxi waiting for you when you return.'

Dory nodded. 'I'm Tyler's assistant,' she offered, but Felicia shook her head.

'I don't care. You're never going to visit here again. It doesn't matter who you are.'

It was true, Dory realised. It didn't matter who she was. Not to these people – they'd hate her regardless. And in a way… it felt strangely freeing.

Any hopes and dreams she'd had about her and Lucas were over now, as much as it hurt to think it. Even if he could forgive her, she would never live this down. Never be welcome at Midfield House again. Never move past this moment. Not while she was in the States.

But that wasn't all. She couldn't work for Tyler now – how could she go back to the office and face him? And that meant that she couldn't keep up the illusion of her perfect Manhattan life any longer.

A weight lifted from her shoulders at the realisation. She'd had enough of pretending, anyway.

She thought of her emergency credit card, tucked in the pocket of her suitcase. This, even her father would have to agree, definitely qualified as an emergency.

It was time to go home.

***

Lucas slammed the library door behind him. 'What the hell, Tyler?'

'Don't you be mad at him,' Cheryl snapped. 'We're not married anymore, remember?'

'Trust me, I know.' And he gave thanks for it everyday. He wasn't the same man who'd married Cheryl, and he never wanted to be that person again. 'So why the charade? Why rope Dory into our family mess?' God, he couldn't think about Dory now. He was still too angry, too confused. He needed to get things straight with his brother, first. Then he'd deal with her.

'Dory?' Cheryl asked. 'You were kissing your *assistant?*'

'I didn't know you were going to be here!' Tyler said, which Lucas thought probably wasn't going to help his case.

'Let me see if I've got this right,' Lucas said, keen to understand what the hell was going on before Cheryl started berating Tyler for kissing another woman. 'You were secretly dating – God, no, engaged to – Cheryl and got photographed. Mum demanded you bring the new girlfriend to visit and, knowing you couldn't bring my ex-wife home for Christmas, you roped your assistant into being your fake girlfriend in return for a plane ticket home for New Year.'

Tyler nodded. 'That's about it.'

97

'You did what?!' Cheryl screeched. 'So what? You've been playing happy families with her all weekend?'

'Look, you two can fight out that part of it later,' Lucas said. 'What I want to know is – when did you tell Dory about Cheryl?' Because if she'd known all along, if she'd agreed to this ridiculous scheme knowing exactly what she was doing… he wasn't sure he could forgive that.

'I didn't,' Tyler said, miserably. 'She figured it out this morning, when she answered my phone when Cheryl called.'

'I was trying to get hold of you to tell you I'd be here tonight,' Cheryl said, defensively. 'I wanted to talk about telling everyone about us. I didn't know you had your other woman here.'

'She's not… it's not like that. She was doing me a favour, so my family could have a nice, straightforward Christmas without all the angst.' Tyler sighed. 'I just didn't want to drive my brother away entirely. Was that so bad?'

Lucas didn't want to sympathise with him, but it was hard not to. He had a point, after all. If he'd known Cheryl was coming tonight, he'd have headed home hours ago. If he'd known she was dating Tyler, he might not have ever come back. It was hard enough leaving his real life behind a few times a year to pretend to be an Alexander again. But despite everything, he loved his parents, even his brother. And he'd always figured that he could give them this much, at least, to keep his family together.

Looked like he and Tyler were more similar than he'd ever wanted to admit.

With a sigh, Lucas dropped into a chair, his anger rapidly fading. 'So this… thing with you two. It's serious? You're really engaged?'

Tyler gave him a sheepish smile. 'I love her, man. I always have. Since the first day I saw her.'

'Oh, baby!' Cheryl launched herself at Tyler, and Lucas looked away into the fireplace.

Since the first day I saw her. How had he not noticed? His brother had been in love with his wife and he hadn't even known.

Even when he figured out that Cheryl most wanted him for his position and prestige – and not at all once he'd changed, once he'd given those things up. And the equally hard realisation that he'd loved what she represented – success, his place, his parents' approval – more than he loved Cheryl herself. Did she really love Tyler? Or was this more of the same?

Did it matter, when Tyler loved her so much?

It did, Lucas knew. But it wasn't his problem to fix. Tyler had what he wanted, at last. And Lucas had his own life to sort out.

Dory hadn't known, not all along. But she'd lied to him that afternoon and kept it secret from him that evening, even as she fell into bed with him. What the hell was he supposed to do with that?

He needed to talk to her, even if he had no idea what to say. Getting to his feet, he started for the door, but stopped at the sound of Tyler's voice.

'Lucas? About Dory… She wanted to tell you, man. She wanted me to tell you, to make things right between us, and when I wouldn't… she was going to.' Tyler winced. 'I might have… well… threatened her. Just a little bit.'

Cold fury rose up in Lucas's chest; all the anger he hadn't felt watching Tyler kiss his ex-wife exploding now at the thought of him threatening Dory. '*What* did you do?' he asked, keeping his fists clenched at his sides. But if his brother's answer didn't satisfy him, he might not be responsible for his actions.

'I told her that if you found out the truth before we left here on the 26th, she wouldn't get her ticket home for New Year.' Tyler glanced down at the floor. 'And, uh, I might have suggested that she wouldn't have a job afterwards either.'

'When was this?'

'A couple of hours ago, I guess. She'd just finished getting ready for the party.'

And she'd come to his room. She'd come to tell him and he'd dragged her into bed.

'Look, tell her I'm sorry, yeah? And the job's still hers if she wants it.' Tyler pulled an envelope with a bow on it from his jacket pocket. 'And give her this?'

Her ticket home. Scowling, Lucas took it. 'I need to talk to Dory. You two… be happy or something.' Lucas yanked open the library door. He was going to fix this mess, once and for all. And then he was taking Dory back to bed, with no secrets between them this time.

***

Dory crammed her belongings into her case in record time, but Felicia still had a cab ready and waiting when she got down the stairs. She'd changed into jeans and a sweater, leaving her burgundy dress on the floor of the bedroom. She was never going to wear it again, and she needed the suitcase space.

There were no lingering goodbyes; Lucas and Tyler were still in the library with Cheryl, and Felicia didn't even feign disappointment about how things had turned out. Dory bundled into the cab and asked for the station, plugging her headphones in the moment they pulled away to avoid having to talk to the driver. The soothing sound of Christmas music reminded her that she was going home. Home, at last.

Things could be a lot worse, she told herself, and almost believed it.

She got lucky with trains and made it to the airport in the early hours. It was Christmas Day and she was going home come hell or high water. Her eyes were scratchy and sore, her whole body ached and she knew that if she stopped moving for a moment she'd start crying, so she kept going.

The airport was eerily quiet for the holidays; she supposed the number of people wanting to fly on Christmas Day itself wasn't huge. Dragging her bag along behind her, she scanned the boards for flight times. The next flight to London left at six a.m. and her luck must have changed because she managed to get a seat on it

100

for less than the limit on her emergency credit card. Checking her bag, Dory headed for security.

But when she got there, she found Lucas Alexander leaning against a pillar in the almost-empty terminal, watching her approach.

Her heart, which had stopped sometime in that hallway with Felicia, started thumping again, blood pulsing in her ears. 'How did you get here?'

'I drove,' he said, as if the last few hours hadn't happened. 'Quicker than the train.'

'I meant… What are you doing here?' Dory let her carry-on bag drop to the ground. Apparently her miserable Christmas Eve wasn't over just yet. She had to deal with the man she'd fallen for, hating her in person, first.

'Catching you,' he replied. 'You forgot these.' He tossed something at her and she caught it, just.

She blinked at the packet in her hand. 'You drove all the way here to give me ginger chews.'

Lucas shrugged. 'You get travel sick. Besides, you left before we could talk.'

'I'm leaving,' Dory said. 'I'm going home, confessing everything and staying there. There is absolutely no need for us to talk.'

'Confessing what?' Lucas asked. 'That you skipped a family Christmas to pretend to be my brother's girlfriend?'

'That I lost my dream job in PR. And my fiancé. And my apartment. That I'm just an assistant now, not the high-flying executive they think I am. And that I'm so broke I had to agree to this stupid stunt just to be able to get home for New Year.' Her skin burned, itching with embarrassment. Shame. God, what were her parents going to say? 'That I used my emergency credit card, the one Dad said only to use in case of near-death, to get a ticket home. And it doesn't matter that I can't afford to fly back to the States because I've got no job to come back for, and I just screwed up the one really good thing that's happened to me this year. You.'

'You're not coming back?' Lucas stepped closer. 'I don't like this plan. And I want to know more about this fiancé.'

'He doesn't matter. He never did.' Dory swallowed around the lump in her throat, feeling tears burning behind her eyes. 'Look, Lucas, I'm sorry. You have to know that. But now… I just want to get the hell out of this. I want to go back to my real life, whatever that's going to be. But I think it's pretty clear it's not going to have anything to do with the Alexander family.'

Lucas shook his head. 'Not good enough. You promised me a date when you got back to New York.'

Was he serious? He'd practically kicked her out of his parents' house himself, before his mother actually had, and now he wanted to take her on a date? What had she missed?

'I spoke to Tyler,' Lucas went on, when it became clear she wasn't going to respond. 'He knows he screwed up, and I know it was a hell of a lot more his fault than yours. So if you still want your job when you get back, you have it.'

'I told you. I can't come back.' The ticket she'd used her emergency credit card to buy was one-way. And even if Tyler came through with a ticket back, even if she still had a job… it was time to tell her family the truth about her life.

'Then I'll have to come with you.'

Dory stared at him, standing there with his arms folded across his chest, watching her steadily. 'Did you eat the mistletoe? Is this some sort of poison-crazy you're talking?' She needed to know. Because something was rising up inside her and it felt an awful lot like hope. She couldn't let that happen if he was crazy and all this was going to fall apart again.

He laughed, and it sounded more carefree than she'd heard from him since they met. 'No, Dory. I did not eat the mistletoe.'

'Good. That stuff will kill you.' She looked up at him, desperation filling her. 'I don't understand what's going on here, Lucas.'

'That's how I've felt since I met you,' Lucas admitted. 'But now, finally, I have some answers. And while I don't like all of them… I can't let them stop me finding out what there could be between us. Learning all the truths about you, instead of the lies. Why you came to New York, what happened to your dream job. What your family are like. Everything. Because somewhere in the craziness of the last few days… I fell for you, Dory. Hard. And I'm not going to let you just disappear out of my life without giving us a real chance.'

'So you're… what? Going to come spend Christmas with my family?'

Lucas shrugged. 'Why not? You were going to spend Christmas with mine, and they're horrible people.'

'You have a point.'

'So I can come?'

'You'll need a…' He held up a boarding pass. 'Ticket,' she finished, lamely. 'We should, I don't know, talk about this.'

'Flight leaves in thirty minutes. We can talk on the plane.' He pulled an envelope from his pocket and Dory recognised the bow. 'And if you do decide to come back, the return part of this is still valid.'

'But—'

Lucas stepped forward, one hand at her waist, and it felt so much more right than it had with Tyler, or anyone before. 'The only question is, do you want to spend Christmas with me? No charade, no lies, just us, your family, some mulled wine and probably cake.'

'Mince pies,' Dory corrected. 'My mum makes the best mince pies in England.'

'You know, I don't think I've ever tasted a mince pie.'

Dory looked up at him, at his bright-blue eyes and cropped hair, at the shoulders she'd cuddled against, the lips she'd kissed and the face she'd fallen for, totally and completely. And she knew, whatever happened next, it would be better with Lucas beside her.

'Well, then,' she said, moving closer into his arms. Maybe things could be okay, after all. 'You'd better come home with me. Everybody should taste a mince pie at least once in their life.'

Lucas flashed her a quick grin, then bent down to kiss her again, hard and fast. 'They have mistletoe in England too, right?'

'Forests full of it,' Dory promised, feeling giddy. This, this was the life she wanted to go home and show her family she was living. A job she liked and a man she adored. But more than that, she wanted to show them how happy she was. 'And I'm going to kiss you under every single bunch we see.'